The Grand Theatre of Cupid

notionpress.com

The Grand Theatre of Cupid

Arun Sugavaneshvar

notionpress
.com

Notion Press

Old No. 38, New No. 6

McNichols Road, Chetpet

Chennai - 600 031

First Published by Notion Press 2016

ISBN 978-81-7511-059-5

CONTENTS

AUTHOR'S NOTE

Love is an adventure transcending popular imaginations that we have read, seen or heard of. It seems rather impossible for any writer to not flirt with the notion of love through his or her words and works. Sometimes, it is like this never ending story of the universe that multiplies and presents itself through different names and species. Love is the language that needs no grammar. No rules whatsoever. None. The one finite and perfect code of existence that makes time redundant. But having said that I know that you will all agree to the pain it may cause as much as it is capable of eternal bliss.

The Grand Theatre of Cupid is a collection of five short stories that will appeal to anybody who is in love, who has been in love and who contemplates on signing up for it (not that you have a choice) anytime soon. I assure you a satisfying concoction of humour, misunderstandings, pain of separation and most of all the magic of love. Not all love stories have happy bye-byes. Not any good ones that I have heard of. Some stories teach us love. Some love stories teach us life.

I wish you all epic love stories in your real life.

Happy reading to you and thank you.

PREFACE

I have been in love more often than I have admitted. I have felt its swelling emotions within me. Love is of many things that I marvel and know very less of. A great many souls of the past have made brave attempts at getting this right. To explain love and its invincible might. What is so difficult? Why is it so elusive to human reason? I can feel it so truly, yet never be able to capture it in the most profound meaning of words.

I guess it's because words are for things that need to be explained. Love is curiously not so. It's inherent in the universe. It's that which is not said but which is known. I am very sure of the fact that it will find you. It will change you. It will show you. It will guide you. It will make you believe.

There is no perfect way to love. No course book on how to fall in love? How to deal with a broken heart? How to get over things that you are unable to? There will be tears. There will be fights. There will be goodbyes. You will sorely miss that someone. Trust me you are going to do alright.

Look around you. It's a symphony of love. A man who went on his knees to propose. A woman who said yes. An intimate kiss. A new mother who saw her first born. A great grandmother who saw her fourth generation. A father who hugs his child to sleep. A brother who gives his favourite toy to his sister who weeps. Those moments with your best friends that got you into trouble. The kindness of a stranger who gives you a lift while stranded. The charity of a meal for the hungry. The heavenly feeling you get after you hear an inspiring piece of music. That moment when your childhood dream is realised. The time your child grows into a great human. That moment when you look back at your life and feel like applauding for yourself. That moment when you know your family is happy and you did fine along the way.

Some love stories are deep, highly contemplative and difficult to hear without secretly crying. But that's the true majesty of love. It's too much to bear. It's too difficult to let go. It's a lot of drama. Love stories are singly the most inspiring not because they have happy endings but because they don't always have. It is to dare to fall in love and take a chance.

I know what happens in war but not what happens in love. No one ever really knows. To be truly loved is such a rare thing. But to love is to be yourself. That's what we truly are any good at. So what is love anyway?

It's the dancing of the stars. It's the infinite dark. It's the vanishing sky. It's the wandering wind. It's the waking sun.

It's you and me.

SINGLE AND (MISS)TAKEN: A WEEK OF REVELATIONS

"Where were you last evening?" buzzed the WhatsApp message from Rachel. The blue ticks had betrayed Richard who was still processing how to answer that question best without starting another argument on the don't you love me anymore? debate of last week. Things were getting a bit rough for the 3-month relationship. The hands holding the roses started realizing that the thorns were hurting.

Richard had forgotten the monthiversary and such sins are unpardonable in the Magna Carta of love. At least that's the brief of our generation. Guys with bad memories shouldn't fall in love or at least have an equally good excuse to surprise the heartbroken one.

When will you start typing…came the next message. Within the next second, there came another text bearing an angry red-faced bugger who startled the sin-maker Richard. Things were getting out of hand. Richard had to do something. The best he could do was buy time, sending the bugger who always grinned sheepishly followed by a smiley that bore a kiss.

"Love you Rach. XOXO," Richard typed hoping that it would somehow invoke Rachel's mercy. But Rachel was typing…for a long time now and that was not a good sign Richard knew. He was kicking himself about why he had forgotten their monthiversary and how his bloody smartphone in which he had stored such priceless data for remembrance had needed to be sent for service after Rachel by mistake, that was well intended, pushed him into a swimming pool while he was on a call with his affair also known as work. It was back in time to receive her grievances.

There were many things that Richard was bad at. First, he was the perfect example of what one would call an absent-minded academician. He was a dreamer of sorts and he believed in keeping things simple and interesting. He adored his books the most. He had a tough time lying. If anyone had looked at him they would for sure recognize him as the modern-day genius merely by gazing at him for a second or so. He was endowed with good looks and an acute sense for fashion, and he had the ability to convince anyone who entered into a verbal argument with him that he was right and more so that they were wrong. The most important evidence of his genius was he believed that being single was a gift that came with an expiry date and very few embraced it. He was the youngest to become a law professor at his own alma mater. He taught logic and believed in it until he found love.

Richard had friends who were less academicians and more romantics. They preferred to enhance their chances of finding their soulmate through trial and error. But Richard was not caught in the web of such illusory distractions not that he didn't fancy woman but just that he was stuck-up with the idea that someone special is already reserved for him which time will eventually bring forth. It's like in the movie inception. Someone plants a thought in your head that might potentially destroy you. In real terms, bugger was waiting for a miracle despite his expertise on logic. Miracles come with an element of surprise and in time of dire need, but they certainly manifest with intricate logic in them sometimes much beyond human understanding.

Richard and Rachel met by chance. Rachel was a philosophy student who had recently come out of a dysfunctional relationship. She vowed not to fall in love ever again. But as the universe would conspire, she met Richard on a Sunday evening at a lecture on spirituality that they both disliked. It was too annoying to a sensible ear they decided. They both walked out through separate entrances and rushed to clear out of the auditorium.

But the untimely spell of monsoon sabotaged their escape plan. They had to wait until the clouds went dry. Richard opened his case of filter cigarettes and set one on fire. He patiently puffed it, while Rachel was gazing at the clouds gulping down a cup of tea procured from the auditorium canteen. Rachel looked around to dispose the paper cup. She decided to loop throw it into a dustbin close to where Richard was standing. Richard watched her closely. The only thing that was shining bright that day was her luck. It landed well into the dustbin. Richard clapped to express his appreciation. She smiled at Richard and took a bow.

The rain was steady and the climate was getting chilly. A while later, she walked across to him and asked for a cigarette. They befriended on a cigarette. She introduced herself and he did similarly. They had so much similar to each other, starting with the annoying lecture they ditched. Slowly the conversation flowed into climate, ill effects of cigarettes, horror movies, abstract ideologies of life and finally about love.

"What do you think about love?" Rachel asked him.

"I try not to think much about it. It's distracting and compelling," he answered and glanced away.

"And you?"

"It's nothing but the hormones having a bad day."

They giggled at each other and puffed away mocking at love.

"I just got out of a relationship. It was painful. I tattooed his name," she added.

"That's a relief," he said.

"Pardon me, I didn't get you," told Rachel.

"I thought the break up was painful. It's a relief to know it was the tattoo," he said and smiled impliedly, conveying the liberating significance of becoming single though the decision to move on leaving behind something you dearly loved would have caused heartache.

For some odd reason Rachel wasn't offended and she laughed it off.

"I guess you shouldn't be worried. I think you handle yourself well. Looping things into the bin and all," he added.

"I am the only one who is single in my gang of friends now" she expressed her grief.

"Well, if you ask me it's not being single that one should be bothered about but about feeling lonely," he logically explained.

"Are you always like this?" Rachel queried.

"Most of the time. Sometimes I try to keep quiet and make a lot more sense like when I am asleep."

"So tell me about your girlfriend. How is she like? How does she handle someone like you?"

"Oh, she is yet to become my girlfriend. She lives in my future. We both are searching for each other and hopefully someone will find the other soon."

"You are an interesting character. Definitely not something I have come across earlier."

"I have been told so. But you have been the most kind so far to put it so politely. I was termed as an 'arrogant a****le' by someone who thought I should be more polite in declining proposals of love. Saying no to someone bubbling with hormones is going to send some delightful comments your way. Though I understand the other person might be disappointed I find it silly to sweet coat something that will potentially cause pain. I tried it once and the girl thought she had to try harder."

"So complex isn't it?" pondered Rachel.

"It's simple. Just that we prefer to complicate it. The mind simplifies things but the heart makes it complex. You want what you can't have but the heart wants what it wants."

The rain had stopped but Rachel wanted the discussion to go on. Richard however bid adieu and left complimenting her once again on the loop throw into the dustbin.

A week had passed and Rachel had got deeper into the habits of lost love. She had kept herself away from WhatsApp and Facebook. They were peaceful times one would have to think. But they gave more time with her depressed self. It led her friends to worry about her absurd behaviour which resembled that of a zombie. So her friends guided her into a rehabilitation of sorts with the help of Facebook. They asked her to log into her account and went on a befriending mode of good-looking friends of friends. You are sure to find people on Facebook even unknown to mankind. So it happened that the zombie amid the chic gang suddenly grew curious over the friend suggestion of Richard. Soon Facebook had got them close enough for a cup of coffee and the rest is history. Richard believed she was the one as she wasn't over bearing as a companion and thought they would make a perfect fit.

The typing…had stopped and the message reached a worried Richard.

"Purple Streak Café at 11 a.m. Be on time. Idiot XOXO," it read. He never understood how someone can take such a long time to type such a short message.

Anyway, he disregarded any further analysis of the same and rushed to salvage what was left of a merciful romantic meet. Rachel was earlier even today despite the fact that Richard reached on time at 11.

"Always late." He knew well he shouldn't argue. He had learned the basics of courting. Apologize even if the other side is wrong.

"Sorry I had actually gone to get this pendant for you. I am so sorry about forgetting yesterday sweetheart. I have been an idiot as you rightly put. Actually a forgetful idiot."

The pendant had a glistening heart and was so beautiful but Rachel wasn't going any soft on him. She proclaimed the penalty for such a forgetful behaviour. A week of celebrating their monthiversary and pampering her with gifts and compliments all the week. That seemed fair given more tearful debates on comparing how other boyfriends behaved could have been worse. No man likes to hear it and no woman likes to not say it.

"Anything for you Rach," he promised and kissed her hand.

He placed the pendant around her neck. She adjusted her hair and asked him how it looked.

"It looks so good. It's got this insane shine that it transmits to you."

She grew red faced again. "So you mean I look shinier only by wearing this and didn't look as good before this."

Richard wanted to eat his words back or at least erase the last few minutes but that too wasn't logically doable.

"Sorry Rach. I didn't mean it that way, all I wanted to say was that it looks really nice on you but I guess I got carried away explaining it."

Tears ran down Rachel's eyes. She sniffed into a wet tissue and looked away from Richard.

"What's happening to us?" she asked him after a brief pause.

"Nothing we are bonding and learning to love each other. It's difficult but doable," he said. She sprang into his arms and hugged him tight.

"Saved by the skin of my teeth. Thank God for my talking skills," he thought to himself. Putting things in perspective was his forte and that was helping but not all the time. Tears beat talking every time and every guy who was in such a situation is a testimony to that.

"Don't ever do this again Richard. I can't bear to see us fight," she said brushing her head against his perfumed denim shirt.

"Well that won't happen if you try reasoning with yourself," he thought to himself.

And sooner than they knew, it was tomorrow. Richard knew he had to be in his best behaviour and think of surprising ways to gift her. He basically wanted to earn her trust and to somehow make her understand that he adores her completely.

Monday

The texts started as early as 5 a.m. even before the alarm slated for 6 got to beep.

"Hey lover what's the plan today evening?"

Richard was way too sleepy to realize the vibration. Then came the phone ringing at 5:30. He wasn't done dreaming yet. Unfortunately for him, he was up till late last night writing his thesis to get his PhD.

Six missed calls within half an hour at last got him up to a very unhappy morning. He picked up the seventh call and asked,

"Who is it?"

"Your ex-girlfriend," came the reply.

"Huh, I am sorry you seem to have dialled a wrong number. I have no ex," he replied and cut the call still keeping his eyes closed and totally disoriented.

Somewhere between going back to sleep and wondering why he has had the misfortune of a wrong call in this early hour his faint intuition recognized the tone of that familiar voice. He jumped up like a spring back in action. He took his phone in a frenzy and reached out to call.

This is it, he thought to himself. He called and called and ultimately he understood that Rachel had become furious as she had declined to accept the calls.

He tried sending texts but they too were unable to get any reply. He hurried and rushed to the bus stop where she would board the bus to her university. She stood as beautiful as a dove in the morning sun. He was sure he was going to be pardoned or else she wouldn't dress this fancy for it was the week of celebration.

But anyway he reached the bus stop and remembered every line he had memorized if he was caught. He had brought with him a small gift that was encased in a glass bottle. One can see deep within it to find the exotic words "My one true love" and a funny sketch of Richard proposing to Rachel and Rachel kissing Richard reminding her of that memorable evening near the beach under a thousand stars staring beyond the evening sky at them.

He sneaked behind her unnoticed like a ninja or at least that was what he thought. It looked really funny for even she knew he was right behind her but she stood showing no sign of care. The gift was sent through a messenger who was a close friend of hers who went gaga over the gift and wished him all success given she heard how he was so unromantic a little while earlier.

"It's not for you. It's for her. So stop blushing. You might put me into more trouble than I already am," said Richard and rushed out completely ninja style similar to the way he entered.

The gift had somehow got them texting once again for she was completely bowled over. She couldn't stop showing her friends the same and claiming to have got the best boyfriend. The first text after their fight was the smiley with tears. Richard was way too confused as to her reaction. If she is mad, she cries and if she is happy, she cries.

Now was she happy or still mad he knew not. She had texted back a picture of her kissing the bottle. Richard felt a sigh of relief.

"So sorry sweety. Honestly was way too tired and didn't recognize it was you."

"This eve we are off to shopping. I am getting you something," Rachel informed like the early morning episode had gone beyond recall.

The evening saw them rush into the Royal Crown clothing store. She picked out a few premium dresses and pushed Richard to try them. Out of the blue there appeared Sarah a childhood friend of Richard along with a guy named Robin. Sarah rushed and hugged Richard leaving Robin to choose his clothing.

"How have you been Richard?"

"Sarah. It's been so long. I have been good and missing your terrifying presence."

"Richard, my childhood sweetheart you still look like I could steal you away. You are a handsome hottie now. Remember those days when we rehearsed the Titanic. I was your Rose and you my Jack."

Rachel was looking at things unfolding before her with complete disbelief and jealousy was stirring its way upward to her eyes.

Richard introduced Rachel as his girlfriend. Sarah looked Rachel from head to feet and started "So you are the lucky one, eh?"

"He is a gem of a guy. Don't miss him. He is hard to find and easy to miss. Many will be envying what you have starting with me," she said with a serious face.

A moment later, she dropped the act and giggled as hard as she can.

"I am sorry. I couldn't resist but see your reaction to such words. But believe me every word I said is true. He truly is a gem of a guy."

Richard couldn't but stare in bewilderment over what was in progress. It was unbelievable. Someone had silenced Rachel for over a minute. Richard soon interfered sensing how Rachel would feel.

"Rach this is Sarah, my childhood friend. A limited edition character. She can be terrifying yet, she is such a sweet person within."

"Richard what are you wearing. Isn't blue your favourite colour?" pondered Sarah.

Rachel had got him a multi-coloured T-shirt which looked fairly good on him but as fate would have it that comment had to be made.

"Richard you look like a peacock," mocked Sarah.

Richard laughed it off while Rachel stared at him for not replying to it. Sarah received a call on her mobile and excused herself from the conversation.

"Go and change it," started Rachel.

"No Rach, this is fine. I like it."

"You don't have to pretend to like it. Your childhood sweetheart said it right. Don't annoy me. Please change."

Richard didn't want to have any meltdown at a public place and so did as told.

Robin in the meantime engaged in a conversation with Rachel after observing what transpired.

"Sarah can be little outspoken. She is like that. I am sorry for the things she said. I really like that T-shirt. I think it looks really good on him. You love him a lot. I can see from your emotions."

Rachel almost felt her eyes swelling up with tears.

"You seem a really nice guy."

"And you seem a really great girlfriend. Actually he is really lucky. I am jealous if it's any consolation," said Robin.

She laughed and blushed a while and asked him to stop complimenting her. Richard walked out and Robin introduced himself as Sarah's friend.

Sarah bid goodbye to Richard and Rachel followed by a wink at Richard before she left with a calm and formal Robin who wished Rachel the best of times with Richard.

All the way back the car was filled with silence. Richard stopped at Rachel's place. They both stayed in it for a while.

"I am sorry about Sarah. That's the way she is."

"Well she seems to know what you like most and asks you out in front of me and you keep mum when she humiliates me. You like the attention you get from her, don't you Richard?" she queried.

"No Rach, not at all. It's been a really long time and yes blue is my favourite colour. But today was about you giving me anything as a token of your love. I don't care what it is. You gave it to me and that is all that matters. It's you that I care about."

"Robin was a lot more sensitive than you are about the feelings of others."

"I am happy he is a good man but I was being diplomatic and that's my friend who was taking a friendly shot at you. You could have very well responded to her out there. Let's not make this day about some bad moments we went through. We both are together. Let's talk about us."

"I have been talking about us all this while if you haven't been listening. Robin said you were lucky to have me," blurted Rachel.

"I certainly am despite the fact that Robin is frequently featuring in our conversation and you seem to have a soft corner for him merely because he took your side. I don't need Robin to tell how lucky I am. I know it myself."

"Now you are blaming me for calling him sensitive while you were hugging and reliving some old Titanic rehearsal flame. Shame on you."

Rachel stormed out. Richard was too emotionally tired in his own way and went back to his place disappointed with the way the evening had ended. Both seemed to have believed that the other was wrong and both waited for the other to initiate further conversation.

The night ended with the crack in the relationship widening a little more. The trust they had in each other was failing. The next morning was rather a peaceful one in terms of text messages and calls but the hearts were at war and there was a silent storm that was ruining a relationship.

Tuesday

Richard was incharge of organizing a high profile academic program at his alma mater. He texted to Rachel, "Held up today. Work calls. Love you. Have a good day." He hoped to receive a reply but there wasn't one. He checked his phone periodically every hour but there was no response. But work had kept him busy enough until late evening.

"Hey Rach just wanted to check on you. Are you still mad at me? Just send me something. Scold me or anything. Just please let me know you are out there." He lamented for over an hour before he got a reply around 10 p.m.

"Had gone out with my friends. I was mad earlier but now I feel a lot better. Sorry, I overreacted. Let's meet up tomorrow. Love you Richard. Good night."

"What? Where to? Tell me about it? I am dying to know. Did you have a good time? You seem to be in a good mood. I am really glad."

Wednesday

There was no response the previous night to his text. The phone buzzed sending in a flurry of texts. They were to meet up to catch the evening show of Mission Impossible 4 at Luxe Theatres. Richard had booked the ticket and was waiting patiently for Rachel. Rachel walked into the theatres and hugged Richard. They had more or less reconciled their differences and Richard believed that things were getting back to normal. They held hands and watched the movie with much delight putting things behind them.

During the interval Richard took to getting refreshments, while Rachel was gleefully talking to someone over the mobile phone way too animatedly.

"Who is it? Rach."

"It's Robin from the other day."

"What? How did he get your number? What's going on?"

"He is the reason today we have both reconciled. We met yesterday. I was waiting for the bus back to my house. He passed by at that time. We caught up and he offered me a drop. We spoke about you so much and I told him what the fight was between us. He was very interested in knowing your character and your likes and dislikes. He is such an awesome friend to hang out with. He gave such good insights on the behaviour of men."

"Okay. I don't recall you telling me you had met him."

"Well he told me that you would be jealous and annoyed if you knew about our meet even if there was nothing going on."

"You could have told. Is that how much you know me? That's all I am asking."

"Now stop asking any more questions. Let's enjoy the movie."

There was not much to enjoy after knowing she was withholding information. Things were getting a lot worse than what Rachel believed in. Richard had grown tired of her ideologies and was certainly not getting the right vibes from Robin.

The movie ended and they walked out but now the silence had become Richard's friend. Rachel was going on about their plans for the next day and nothing was registering in his head. He felt betrayed and in a way insecure.

Thursday

They met at the Purple Streak Café and they embraced each other. Richard had reached there earlier and was seen to be in deep contemplation. He regretted he had changed a lot and that he was transforming into someone else he never wanted to be. Richard had become more silent than before. Rachel sensed it and enquired whether he felt alright. He said it was nothing and went about ordering. She showed the pictures taken on the other the day at the friend's night out. Robin featured in it frequently to upset him further.

He walked out feigning that he had to take a call. Rachel had gone to the washroom. When she was back she found a gift package that read "To the one I love from Robin." Robin had seen that Richard was out roaming. He made sure that Richard was back to see the gift by prompting the waiter to inform him. The gift was too huge to hide. Rachel was shocked herself and to her dismay Richard returned to see this.

"Now what's this?"

"Richard, I swear this is not what it looks like. I didn't know he would do such a thing."

Richard left without saying a word. Rachel tried convincing him otherwise. But he was left in his own world of wondering whether he was right to have ever gotten into a relationship and changing so wildly and losing his happiness for petty reasons. He had become everything he mocked at while his friends were in a relationship. He couldn't handle what was going on. He has been the one who always initiated the compromise in the relationship. But he knew within his gut that he had taken it too far.

Rachel tried contacting Richard but he wasn't responding. She called Robin and fired him for such a foolish and cheap behaviour but Robin kept patient without giving any response. He was embraced by sorrow in his own way that he couldn't explain. He felt the attraction. So he acted on it though he knew he was doing something stupid. This was the ultimate test for their relationship to survive. The only words Robin had to say to Rachel were "I am very sorry for what I have done. It is not what it looks like."

Rachel yelled back giving no time for him to explain his end.

Friday and Saturday

In the following 2 days, Rachel was making many fervent attempts to apologize and try to reach out to Richard but Richard showed no sign of responding or making any contact. Rachel had lost all faith. This was too much. There was no fault of hers and she felt that Richard was acting too smart. She texted Robin and Richard and told them that she wanted to meet them both.

Sunday

The Purple Streak Café saw the three of them walk in one after another as if they were at a mourning.

Rachel started loud and clear "Richard, I don't think we work. You are not sensitive to my feelings and you treat me like I am an option. So we can't be together anymore. So I have decided to call it quits."

Richard broke his silence, "Thank you so much. I dumped you 2 days back. I am here to pity that poor bugger and give you a confirmation."

Rachel grew furious and blurted, "Robin is sensitive to my feelings and is such a wonderful person who emotionally supports me. I think we will get along well and in the due course we might just make the perfect couple."

Robin stopped Rachel and asked, "Are you sure you broke up with him?"

"Hell, yes" replied Rachel.

"In that case will you go on a date with me Richard?" asked Robin.

LATE FOR THE BEST FRIEND'S WEDDING

"It's already late. Are you done sightseeing in there? Now walk out of the bloody toilet? I am warning you. I am almost out of control here you germinator," screamed Rishi.

"What the f**k are you screaming about yaar?" mumbled a half awake Bai who adjusted his shorts that had lowered down revealing one side of his big fat butt.

"I think it's the paneer butter masala from yesterday that is screaming," responded an annoyed Rishi.

Buddy was uninterested in the conversation as he was maniacally changing channels on the TV that promptly informed that the subscription had lapsed and that only the regional channels were available.

"This is horrible man. I am going to call the room service and tell them to pay their subscription. What kind of service is this? We have paid for the room, the services and allied accessories right? I have not seen this poor service since…(he thought for a while) well for a long time now. What do you say guys?"

Rishi looked at him and stared. "There are more urgent matters that need attention. So shut up and order us some tea or coffee" he moaned and went back to hammering the loo door cursing Sonu.

"Ask them if they have any biscuits or tea cakes to go with," Bai instructed with his eyes still closed.

The Night Star lodge was not the most aesthetic of places to be at or comfortable for that matter. But they were unable to get into any other place as they arrived in the very last minute to attend the marriage of their college mate Farhan.

Sonu, Farhan, Rishi, Bai and Buddy were last benchers, which meant they shared a bond that lasts a lifetime. Farhan had migrated back to Chennai, his hometown, after graduation but these five had a riotous 3 years reading commerce in their free time when they were done dating, partying and flirting. The one thing common to all of them was their fear of family. Whenever any one of their families visited, they would behave in such a manner that even Forrest Gump would look like a bad guy.

But as life would have it, they had to part ways by accidently clearing their semesters with massive help from office clerk Jagan whose cycle turned into three Nanos at the end of those 3 years. An entrepreneur is someone who attains his target by doing every mistake imaginable in a way that he looks like a rockstar was their learning at the end of their 3 years. The only most productive venture they ever did was to start a dating consultancy which of course was very successful for them in terms of them transforming from being a nobody to becoming the most sought after love gurus. Love advice is the easiest thing to do. It's almost like philosophy which is popularly explained as, searching for a black cat in a dark room where there is no cat.

Sonu had finished. He appeared exhausted and the words came out feebly "It's definitely the paneer butter masala. I need some ice to sit on." Bai giggled as he prepared for opening his eyes and giving his darshan to the morning.

"Are you sure you flushed properly?" enquired Rishi.

"Yes, but I advise you should wait sometime for the air to clear out."

He took Sonu's deodorant and sprayed it frantically inside the loo, keeping his head away and soon rushed to liberate himself. Buddy was unable to reach the room service, and he was completely flustered with the way things were going on for him. He slammed the door behind him and bolted to ask for justice. Two floors below the reception lay empty. He walked about until a young chap went behind the desk and started looking for something.

"Hey what do you guys think of yourself? I am from room 21. I don't see you have a good customer-centric service. The TV isn't working. The room service number isn't being picked up. This is such a poor service, and I am planning to complain about it. Who is incharge here?" he screamed.

"I am new to the place myself. You should ask someone who works here."

"Then, who are you?"

"Oh, I am a thief from nearby. This lock won't budge. Can you help me here?"

"What? Thief...thief...," shouted Buddy.

"Even I can't hear you. Now shut up and help me." The thief raised a small knife threatening the bejesus out of Buddy.

Buddy was in complete panic. He went around and helped fearing for his life. Can this day get any worse? he thought to himself. Soon to his rescue came the office cleaning boy who saw this and reported the same to the nearby shop owners. They rushed and held both Buddy and the thief and started thrashing them before Buddy could say anything.

Buddy was royally beaten-up before the cleaning boy could recognize him and ask him what he was doing there. Buddy narrated what had happened, and the thief evidenced further to what he was saying. Buddy went back to room 21, his body aching in places that can't be revealed and he knew his stars were in troubled waters as the astrologer had predicted. He vowed to keep quiet as whatever he was doing was resulting in him becoming the victim.

He knocked thrice before Sonu opened the door to see Buddy who resembled like he had just walked out of a wrestling match.

"Hey, what happened?" enquired a concerned Sonu.

Buddy narrated his sorrow-filled tale as to how the brave seeker of justice in terms of customer satisfaction was coerced to committing a robbery and was beaten-up on mistaken identity.

"That is completely unfortunate Buddy. Let's go complain to whoever is incharge here."

"I am not complaining anymore," withdrew Buddy and opened his first-aid kit to find some Dettol and pain-relieving balm.

"So by any chance did you order us that coffee after that debacle?" asked an insensitive and immensely fat Bai who was now trying to do a lady's push-up with much difficulty.

Rishi walked out and Buddy went in to freshen up and get ready. Bai followed after Buddy. The wedding was to take place the next day. So they had sufficient time to do some shopping and meet Farhan before the wedding and torment him about giving up his bachelor life. They had also planned for a bachelor party.

It was 9 in the morning, and they walked down to the canteen hoping that nothing else would go wrong. The canteen was buzzing with crowd in terms of flies scouting for food. The tables were cleared and the owner of the lodge came to them and apologized for what had happened in the morning. He offered them a complimentary breakfast and 10% off on the room rent. The faces soon glowed after hearing such glorious words of redemption except for Buddy who was unable to smile as his jaw ached if he moved it any swiftly.

Breakfast was served. They decided to stuff themselves given the fact that it was complimentary. The food was not great but it was complimentary, the most compelling reason to hog anything that was dead and cooked. They had hired a car to travel and shop. They decided to do some self-driving and believed that the GPS would take them to their desired destination. The previous night had seen incessant rainfall and diversions were installed throughout the arterial roads. The four were blissfully boarding the Honda City unaware of such a situation.

Farhan had made occasional calls to them and had enquired their plans and advised them to be careful. He gave them his Chennai mobile number and asked them to call him if they needed any assistance. He had asked them to join him for breakfast but they wanted to explore and since it was a short trip they decided to meet him by late afternoon.

There is a very curious thing about Chennai traffic. It's like the relative who gate crashes into our home without notice. It hardly comes but if it comes, it hardly leaves.

So, they were stuck just a kilometre away from the lodge for over an hour. The route was a bit dodgy but the GPS and some considerate men directed them nearer to T.Nagar, the hub of shopping. One can come here and shop and be lost for 2 days without food or sleep. Everything glitters and your wallet shivers. Cheap prices, good quality and a world by itself. You wouldn't know what to buy and what to leave. Always a discount on anything you buy. The best place to understand the aspirations and economic pulse of the middle and lower middle class.

One cardinal rule: You don't go to shop in T.Nagar on a weekend or a day before any festival day. So what happens if you do? You can't get in or if you manage to get in, you can't get out. The crowd will take you into a shop of their desire and drop you out elsewhere. That's the level of maddening crowd that comes there. And if you bring a car hoping there is parking, amen to that.

They reached the bazaar of bazaars. It was all negotiations and closing deals. If you wanted to learn something about business, it's better to walk out of your MBA class and spend a month roaming these streets. You might learn a lot more about that black box in the consumer's head they teach you about.

The four had a tough time fighting their way through a rash undisciplined buying frenzy. They parked their car at a corner of a no parking zone where other fellow cars were fearing the arm of law, while their owners were striking immensely lucrative deal for half the actual price. The irony is the fact that cars which are worth a few lakhs were left unattended to cater to appeasing hurt egos that couldn't negotiate a deal with the supermarket guys who did business on a fixed price.

They searched and enquired for the best apparel shop in the locality. They spent hours finding the right fit and colour to woo people at the wedding. It had been a few hours before they emerged victorious and completely drenched in sweat starting to wonder they had been at the gym or shopping. They walked out of the Royal Blazers shop that had given them a 10% discount, and right across they found a shop owner in the process of displaying a sign board that read 40% discount on blazers and they could feel all the happiness of an economically prudent purchase go in the drains. They felt betrayed as the shops had strict non-refundable and no exchange policies.

They felt like losers until they saw their car clamped and prepped for being towed. They felt irreversibly frustrated thereafter. It was a series of unfortunate events perpetuating in a manner only known to the Lord of ill luck which had befriended them. Another 700 was spent on purchasing the mercy of a highly irresponsible traffic personnel.

They returned hungry and tired to a restaurant that had a menu that ran into 20 pages that it would take a good 15 min to read and pick a food at that late scorching afternoon. Last night it had rained, but today it was all sun. The waiter walked closer and offered to take an order, if they were ready.

"So how long do you take to serve food here?" queried Bai who felt life forces draining out of him.

"It primarily depends upon how long you take to order them in the first place?" replied the waiter.

Buddy looked up at such an answer and giggled within. Bai was completely annoyed at such a reply yet still he remained calm and asked Rishi to order soon.

"So, we will have two plates of veg fried rice, two plates of veg noodles and one kadai paneer."

"Sorry sir, we don't have veg fried rice. It will take us another half an hour to make. Veg noodles is not available, as it has been sold out. Kadai paneer is available though."

"You gave us the menu which was ultimately a short story book and I read it patiently despite disturbing price specifications and you say you don't have most of the items I have ordered. So what do you have?"

"We have meals sir. It's the most economic and will be served fast given your rush for food."

"Four meals then," blurted Bai getting uneasy with the developing conversation.

"Alright sir. Then, let me repeat your order for you."

"I am pretty sure of what you have ordered for our lunch Mr. Waiter," said Sonu.

"So would you like to have regular water or bottled water?"

"What's the difference?" pondered Sonu.

"Bottled water is mineral water and regular water is corporation water which we claim to have treated well for consumption."

"Three 1 litre bottles then," Bai ended the debate.

The meals were served. They definitely were tasty and filling and the bill proceeded to the table of the four, well concealed in a black leather jacket hardcover board which gave it a very holy touch.

"The scary truth lies within," said Sonu, waking his wallet to pay up.

He opened it and it was scary indeed. It was Rs. 300 in all but what was scary was the charge of the bottled water was more than the combined price of four meals.

"There must be some mistake. It says 150 for three mineral water bottles and the MRP says otherwise," said a puzzled Sonu.

"Well that's the law I can charge a little more than the MRP for the aesthetic experience I give you. Scary truth eh?" grinned the waiter who walked away with 20 more rupees as his tips apart from the service charge and tax that were already printed on the bill.

They walked out still debating on the legal stand over this issue and reached the car and decided to meet up with Farhan. A good-looking chick had walked past them. An indigo sleeveless top with a white skirt is distracting, adding brunette, 5' 6", a sparkling smile and twinkling eyes with it is magic, adding the right amount of voluptuous with flawless skin is just inhumanely perfect. They were lost for words and the thought of being overbilled had completely escaped the mind. Out of sight out of mind, the one thing that doesn't apply to beautiful women.

Sonu tried calling Farhan. His mobile has been switched off or is not reachable at the moment, the sad lady from the service provider promptly informed. Buddy suggested that they get back to the lodge and rest for a while before they set out to meet Farhan. The other three unanimously agreed, given their tedious journey from Delhi was on an unreserved train and they hadn't slept well the previous night.

All four woke up again much to their dismay around 7 p.m. They had been sleeping for over 4 hours now. They tried contacting Farhan again. But the sad lady had got only sadder. They tried reaching him by sending messages through Hike, WhatsApp and some absurd Instagram pics which they had taken at the trial room at the Royal Blazers shop. But there was no response for more than an hour. They remembered Farhan telling that the marriage hall was at Santhome a place very close to Marina beach. So they planned on heading towards the marriage hall and finding out from someone out there.

They got ready as soon as possible and boarded the vehicle and the GPS came alive charting their course of travel. Well it was a straight route from Nungambakkam via Gemini flyover and Dr. Radhakrishnan Road right to Marina beach. They had been worried why Farhan had not been responding or had not taken notice that his mobile had switched off.

They resembled toddlers who were amazed by the night glitter of the city. It looked so charming, bright and one would easily fall in love with the evening look of Chennai. It was the shine of a new bride and had an informal grandeur to it that one could easily connect to. All was well and the four were proceeding towards Marina beach. It was a weekend and the beach was still alive. Scores of vehicles had been parked and it was almost 8:30, and the vehicles were slowly parting ways without any heart carrying their tired passengers and granules of beach sand as a remembrance of that beautiful evening.

Rishi suggested to drop in and look around before they marched on to Santhome. The GPS had informed that just a kilometre ahead was the Bright Future Marriage Hall where they wanted to enquire first. So they debarked and ventured into the beach. There were silhouettes of couples hugging, holding hands and some secretly kissing near and far and that virgin night was a fresh canvas for many abstract romantic portraits.

The waves were a little rough. They managed to get themselves wet much above their loins and took selfies that were promptly updated on FB which failed to gather any likes except their own. (If only Facebook had a dislike button.) They gorged on some lip smacking tasty bajjies from the shops that were dishing out plate after plate to insatiable customers.

It was 9:15 already and they moved out of the beach towards Santhome. The Santhome Church was decorated with multicoloured lights which caught their attention from a kilometre away. It was surreal. It looked majestic and pious in ways only a servant of God would know. They went further, and there on their left next to that giant board that read Bright Future Marriage Hall, they entered. The celebrations of the previous wedding had just concluded and the decorations for the next were on. They enquired around and learned that it was the place where the reception would be held and that Farhan was held up with the pre wedding formalities along with his relatives at his place.

They were disappointed that they were unable to meet Farhan but dinner was served to the relatives and friends who had boarded lodges nearby to take part in the wedding the next morning. The four had their fill of a delicious traditional dinner and walked out reminiscing that this was the last day of the bachelor life of one of their best mates.

Bai was worried that they couldn't have a bachelor party. He recommended that they go to a bar nearby and have a drink as a toast to Farhan. But the other three voted against it.

"Bright Future Marriage Hall, what an ironic way to name a marriage hall," mocked Sonu.

They blissfully started on their voyage back to the lodge. It was around 10 in the night and the traffic had diminished from a four-column traffic to just random cars driven at a dangerous pace. The signals couldn't do much but just blink at erring road racers. They slowly drove close to the Marina beach and turned towards Gemini flyover where a few hundred metres away, they were stopped unexpectedly.

It was the police personnel during their random checks. They were questioning a girl who looked very similar to the girl they had jaw dropped gazing earlier late afternoon. She turned around and it was her. The jaw dropping continued. Why is she questioned, they were puzzled. They were asked to blow at the alcohol level finder.

"It's shocking to see youngsters these days at such late hours driving without intake of alcohol," complimented the inspector.

The constable whispered something in the ear of the inspector. The inspector gazed at the four men and asked for their ID proof. The four were getting ready for their next unfortunate event. This was going to be big they thought to themselves. They handed over their ID proofs and their visiting cards. The car number was noted, and they were being thoroughly checked. After verification, they were called forward.

"Her name is Sana," the inspector introduced the woman to the four. They carefully nodded without making any swift moments that revealed their joy of introduction.

"I need you to drop her carefully at her residence. She lives in Nungambakkam. I am holding you guys responsible if anything goes wrong. Remember I have your contact info, and I will find you and put a bullet to your head if you guys try anything funny. Once you drop her you ask her relatives to talk to me. You got me?" he roared.

"Yes sir," they all said like in a chorus. She obliged and hesitantly walked to the car and got in.

"It's late night and I am trusting you guys. I believe the youth of our country are not all bad and irresponsible. She needs your help at this late hour. So act like gentlemen," he appealed to their good side.

They agreed and travelled in complete disbelief. Her presence was so fragrant. They had all been tired after the evening and weren't looking their best. A silence had caught hold of them. An untold joy brought smiles to them. Sonu was driving and she sat beside him. Her hands tucked in towards her body and she looked straight.

Bai took out his comb and combed his hair or what was left of it now that it enhanced the look of his baldness. Rishi was wondering what to speak to break the silence. Such a perfect looking chic beside them in the same car. Buddy was praying to thank almighty and was almost sure that this broke the streak of unfortunate events that had befriended them earlier. They all felt lucky.

All of a sudden unexpectedly she spoke, "Guys, I need your help. I am trying to meet my boyfriend. My parents are against our marriage."

They all looked at her with more sorrow than ever. They all grew an imaginary beard marred by frustration. It was all over. All their dreams and aspirations of flirting and having a chance to get to know her were futile. She was taken and they knew it was a far shot within. The gentlemen in them took over.

"Alright," started Rishi. "How can we help you?"

"I need to get to my boyfriend. He will figure out what to do."

They took her to her boyfriend. He looked like a crazy drug addict who grew funny hair. Their sorrow was beyond words.

Bai secretly cried, "Why do such good-looking women choose such guys?"

Rishi agreed, "What hurts more is knowing such a fellow could get her?"

"And we call ourselves love gurus," mocked Buddy.

Sonu walked towards them. He couldn't bear to see them hugging for so long unmindful of their presence though his reasons were not only that.

They parted and the boyfriend thanked them for their gesture.

"Guys you are the best kind of gentlemen I have ever met. Thank you so much. Can I ask you for one last favour?" requested Sana.

Sonu nodded in agreement but deep within he kicked himself for doing such a gesture. The boyfriend spoke to the inspector feigning to be her relative.

"We have to leave immediately. Even my parents are against our union," said the boyfriend. He had no clue what to do and the girl trusted him and was holding his hands like it was stuck with Fevicol.

The love gurus were reminded of their good old days when they fought to help lovers. They decided to help them at any cost. But Buddy warned them that it might lead to something more unfortunate. They were overcome by their yesteryear memories. Both the boy and the girl were of legal age to marry and make their own choices.

Rishi handed over the gift they had got for Farhan. An open ticket for the couple to Jammu and Kashmir for their honeymoon. Buddy, Bai and Sonu hesitantly consented. The boyfriend hugged them and thanked them.

They had not in their worst of dreams thought of getting a hug from that fellow whose jeans fell off every five minutes revealing his torn boxers, and he called them "Bro" every once in a while like he belonged to some other civilization.

They dropped them at the airport and bid farewell.

Sonu looked at her and said, "You look beautiful (after a pause)…together I mean."

"Here, take this as my gift for your big help," she handed over a beautiful blue mermaid pendant that held a heart in its hands. They refused initially but she insisted.

They waved and left to live a life they had dreamt of. The four returned back to the car and slowly drove content with what they had done in a way. We were gentlemen, they pacified themselves. They felt like it was a déjà vu of their college days.

"Farhan would have loved it. I wish he was here with us," said Sonu.

Farhan called them exactly when he was thought of.

"Think of the devil and there he is," proclaimed Sonu.

Farhan asked them to meet him back at the marriage hall.

They reached the Bright Future Marriage Hall where Farhan was waiting to welcome them. They got out of the car and Farhan hugged each one of them.

"I know it's been long dude," said Rishi.

"So shall we go for that bachelor party now at least?" asked a joyous Bai.

They sat at the Believer Bar and drank wildly. Farhan said he had to stay sober and ordered a lemonade. Bai and Rishi started an impromptu jive. They looked really goofy. Just then Farhan received a call that brought tears to his eyes.

"Is my dance that bad? Farhan is in tears," asked Bai unaware of the situation.

"No guys, the marriage has been cancelled," said an evidently shocked Farhan.

"What are you saying?" asked a worried Sonu.

"Well, she didn't like me apparently. She is in love with someone else. I really liked her man," he sobbed uncontrollably.

"Shit happens man. We are there for you," said Bai. "More the reason to drink now," he added.

"I even gifted her my family heirloom, the lovely blue mermaid," informed Farhan.

Buddy had gift wrapped the mermaid to be gifted to Farhan and his to be. He put his whiskey back on the table and felt it in his pocket. The four looked at each other briefly withholding their company.

"What is her name?" Rishi hesitantly asked Farhan.

"Sana," the word unfortunately sounded.

THE ACCIDENTAL DIVORCE

The wall in the hall was having a bad day. It stood naked stripped of the beautiful photos of the couple at apartment 26. There were broken glass pieces strewn in the hall. The pictures were still a pretty thing to look at despite them losing their spot of importance. The marriage had collapsed.

"It's over between us, Aditi. I can't live with such a drama queen. I did not sign up for this," Aditya yelled.

Aditi was packing patiently without responding. It was around 10 p.m. The cuckoo that was housed within the clock had brought it to their notice. It retreated as soon as it saw the mood outside and knew it was curfew time. Aditya called his parents and informed them of his decision to quit from the 8-month-old marriage. They were worried that their son was in haste and certainly in complete error to make such a decision. They tried to talk him out of it but he had made up his mind.

Aditya loosened his neck tie and went over to the fridge to grab a bottle of chilled water to rejuvenate his dry throat. It had been immensely utilized to talk things that were utter nonsense. Some filth, some recollection of troubled past and some unconventional and illusory prediction about his wife's future conduct.

Aditi came out from the bedroom with the travel bag. She then walked to the door and opened it. Aditya looked at her with disgust.

"Now what is this drama? Leaving? Do you want me to call a cab?" queried Aditya in a rough tone that was still unforgiving.

"I think you should call the cab or whatever that suits you."

She threw the bag out and looked at him.

"Leave now. You are really worried of late for illusory reasons. We are unable to have a single conversation without being cynical to each other. I know you are not this guy. Hope you take time to think about us and that things return to normal. Call me once you are calmer," said Aditi.

"What? Are you asking me to leave? How dare you?" retaliated Aditya.

"That is just the wisest thing I have done in the last month. This is my dad's bequeath to me. So it's technically my place," claimed Aditi.

"Fine. You won't see me again. You just sent away the best thing that ever happened to you," said Aditya storming out of the apartment thrashing the water bottle to the ground.

The whole B flat was awake slowly peeking out of their respective apartments to catch some of the action. Aditya swiftly walked with a bruised ego mumbling words to himself. Now all eyes turned towards Aditi. She was the bad one they all decided referring to her daring act.

"Sorry for the disturbance and all the yelling. Good night to you all," she said and excused herself.

It was 7 in the morning and there was no sign of life from apartment 26.

Kokila her jealous neighbour was spreading exaggerated inputs on yesterday's fight. She along with a few of her loyal comrades marched and rang the bell at apartment 26. There was no one answering the door.

"I think that girl could have done something stupid. Suicide or something. These youngsters these days are not knowing how to handle things in relationships or how to run a family. They are weak and pathetic," she announced.

"Yes only last week I read that a girl had taken her life due to some fight with her spouse," informed another. They were the gossip girls of their apartment.

"Do you think I should call the police or break open the door?" enquired Kokila.

"How about I open the door for you?" suggested Aditi who had just come back from her morning jogging session.

The entire gang was dumbstruck and in shock. Aditi smiled and welcomed them inside asking if they preferred to have some hot drink.

"No dear. We were worried that you might be in a devastated state after yesterday's episode with your husband."

"For you everything is like a serial. Isn't it aunty?" said Aditi.

"No, no, no, I meant the fight. So what happened, tell us," pestered Kokila.

"Sorry aunty that's between me and my husband. I don't think it is right to divulge anything about the same. We will sort things out."

"No dear we can give you some advice on how to go about."

"Thanks for your concern aunty but I will handle this," Aditi replied with confidence.

After emptying a few tumblers of coffee, the gang left the apartment 26 and went on their way disappointed unable to extract any information about the fight.

"Look how stubborn she is. After last night she behaves as if nothing has gone wrong. She is not even sad that her husband has left her. I have a strong feeling that she is the reason for her husband to leave," proclaimed Kokila among her comrades.

Aditi soon got ready for office and left. After a usual day of work, she went back home all alone still waiting for a reply from Aditya. But it was far from what was about to knock at her doors. Aditya had sent her a divorce notice. Aditi had hoped he would take time to reconcile. Days passed by faster than one could notice. She kept her routine and hoped Aditya would see the stupidity of giving up on a relationship based on untrue events.

The hearing at the court had commenced a month later. The judge asked Aditya the reason for filing for divorce.

"I can no longer put up with her. She is always trying to find a way to torture me. She emotionally harasses me. The problem with her is that everything has to go the way she wants it to. I have no say in it. She does not respect me and treats me like I am her servant. She has a high paying job and so she no longer feels the necessity to consult me on family-related issues. She was not like this before. I fell in love with the wrong person. She has duped me. Only now do I see her for what she truly is."

The judge turned to Aditi to ask her version.

Aditi started, "He is the only man I trust after my father. My father is no more. He is all the family I have. I still am in love with him. I share every little thing with him. We had a financial crunch and we were unable to pay bills. So I went for a job to help our family. It gave us more comforts and it gave much needed security. But all of a sudden I was asked to leave it without good reason and thereafter he has been really acting strange when I declined. I wanted to be independent and the guy I fell in love with would have supported me through every step. We had little fights over this job matter and eventually it had spilt into every conversation we have had. It has left him with disgust and it has left me helpless."

The judge then asked Aditya to consider reconciling with Aditi as she has clearly expressed her desire to live with him. The discussion had taken them to revisit what had led them to the court applying for divorce. Almost a month and a half ago, it all started when Aditi had stayed back at office to work, while Aditya was left alone on the eve of his birthday.

"Hey, Aditi. It's already late. Where are you? Is there no one to take care of your work just this evening?"

"It's already late and kind of important Aditya. I am the only one who knows about this. I really have to go now. Will see you soon."

"Hey, Aditi… Aditi…" She hangs up the call. Aditya calls her after an hour but she does not pick up the call.

He was hoping that there was some kind of a midnight surprise that Aditi had planned. He believed her to be feigning that she was held up with work. So, he was all set and patiently waiting to enjoy his surprise. It was midnight, he was eagerly looking at the door almost sure she would walk in anytime. He checked his mouth odour. The new mouth freshener had a strong scent. He liked it. All the TV commercials had made a believer out of him. It was 12:01, his mind started questioning her arrival and then gradually to whether she had remembered. He hoped that he would at least be called and wished if she was actually held up at work. He stared at his mobile browsing through all apps randomly and even through play store as if someone could send a message through that, eventually updating all his apps after their long pending reminders. It was quarter past 1. Messages from friends who had insomnia had reached him promptly. People he never spoke to after school and college performed their social ritual but his love had forgotten his important day. He had lost his enthusiasm and was dejected beyond words.

The Aditi he knew would have never missed such a thing. She made sure he felt special, and he made sure she felt likewise. She was being drawn more and more into work. He just sat on the red bean bag that had lost all of its initial charm and which was now ready to lie flat when any human mass was placed on it. He stared at the ceiling as the fan made its circles setting the cobwebs nearby to unstable jolts. They were barely hanging on. Tears rolled down his eyes but he wiped them swiftly and dozed off in the midst of all his dejections on the bean bag. The morning alarm woke him at 6. He struggled to get his ass off the bean bag that was now well ironed into the deep pits almost at par with the floor. He looked around to see if Aditi had come.

She was absent and the mobile had no news of her return. He left for his morning jog. He got back after an hour and found that the door was closed and bolted on the inside. Aditi had come. He rang the bell. To his surprise, a young man must be in his early twenties opened the door and welcomed him. Aditi was making tea. She had already gotten ready for a second round at work. She introduced the young chap as Krish the new employee and her colleague at the Advertising Department who offered to drop her back. Aditya walked in still wondering how she had no clue what day it was. He got ready and left without even having his breakfast.

"Adi, aren't you having your breakfast?" asked Aditi.

"No, I have an important meeting. I am already running late" he informed and bolted to his car even before Aditi could walk to him and give him a hug.

She soon left wondering how he never hugged her wishing her a good day at work. Throughout the day Aditya was found restless and he was unable to focus on his work. He returned early that day and spent the rest of the day reliving his marriage through their wedding CD. It made him feel alright until the call came from Aditi. He hoped this time she had remembered.

"Adi, I am super happy. Guess what. I had such good response to my pitch. All my hard work had paid off."

"That's great to hear Aditi. Will you be…," he started before being interrupted by Aditi.

"And one more thing Adi. I am sorry I couldn't inform you earlier. I am on my way to Bombay. It was unexpected. My boss has asked me to go directly and pitch it before the clients. I had to buy stuff outside and rush to the airport. I can sense my promotion making its way towards me. Everyone is jealous here. So tell me you were saying…," she enquired.

"No, I hoped we could go out for some dinner but anyway enjoy your trip. Be safe and take care."

"Why all of a sudden you planned for dinner?"

"Well, mum and dad are coming. Today happens to be my birthday. I just hoped I could treat you to a good dinner and spend some quality time with the entire family."

There was a long pause after that. Aditi was completely shattered. She had forgotten his special day. She was annoyed with herself. All the happiness from her successful pitch had disappeared without trace.

"Aditi…Aditi…are you there? I am unable to hear you. I am losing you," yelled Aditya thinking it was a network issue.

"No, no. I am here Aditya. I am really sorry Adi. I can't imagine how I had forgotten your birthday. I… I…," she stammered.

"It's alright Aditi. Take care. Call me once you reach. All the best for your pitch. Bye," he said and terminated the call abruptly unable to control his frustration. He switched off his mobile. Aditi tried dialling him once again but the phone was switched off. She knew he was totally pissed.

"A very happy birthday. I am very lucky to have you in my life. I am really sorry I had forgotten such an important day. I know you are mad at me and you have every reason to. I promise, I will make it up to you once I am back. Million, trillion, zillion kisses and hugs to you. Love you Aditya. Muaah," read Aditi's text message.

The next 2 days were more mechanical. Aditya and Aditi were prisoners of their work and most of the time the only thing healing or actually keeping their dejection at bay was their work. Aditi had called him time and again but Aditya refused to pick her call and sent her texts informing of him being busy with work. He enquired about her pitch and kept it like a conversation between two professionals. She was worried but her pitch and her promotion were on line. She did a fine job and returned 3 days after buying some expensive gifts for Adi. Aditya was nowhere to be found. His mobile was switched off. Aditi called his parents. But they were not sure of his whereabouts. She then rang up his office. They informed that he had gone on leave for a week. She sent text after text hoping it would elicit a reply. But there was no response, and the mobile had just the same reply from that lady with her clean phonetic response informing that the mobile was switched off. Aditi was puzzled and didn't know what to do.

A day later, she received a message that informed her that he was out on a trip with his friends. It did not disclose where but just that he will be back in a week's time. Her heart was not at work. She clearly understood the toll her absent mindedness had taken on their relationship. She moved in and out of office without any happiness or will to perform. Aditi's birthday was on September 18. It was September 17. He still wasn't home. She knew why and he wasn't due to return for another 2 days.

Mahi, Yuva and Aditya were best buddies in college. Mahi took charge of his family business, while Yuva was between jobs. Aditya was the one who worked his ass off to get to such a respectable level in his career. He was the manager at the Southpole ice cream company. It was his dream to have his own ice cream company. But as fate would have it, his financial situation never improved to provide him with such an opportunity to live his dream.

He fell in love with Aditi and married her while still at college against his parent's wishes and that had changed a million things.

Aditya intentionally had not informed Aditi. But he felt he needed a break and she needed to feel how he felt. They had gone for a week long holiday trip to Ooty and Kodai which are beautiful hill stations in Tamil Nadu. The splendour and the magnificence of the dew-drenched mountains are curtain raisers for how heaven could actually be. The blinding mist and the chilling wind sends one's senses into a whirlwind of emotions much to be compared to that of an ephemeral experience. They zoomed around the hairpin bends on which clouds sat on and reached the top of the hill while it was still chilly around 10 a.m. in the morning. They checked into a resort and fell tired after having a late brunch into the folds of a warm blanket. They reminisced about their college days. It was pure delight to relive those memories.

Aditya told Yuva and Mahi about the frustrations of a married life and how his ambition will never come to light before he is 40. Yuva stayed single after many failed attempts at being in a stable relationship much like his habit of being between jobs. Mahi married into wealth. He married the daughter of one of his father's business partner. It was an arranged union for aggregating wealth.

"It is like there is no more me or mine. It's all hers. I have to think like two people and behave without trampling on emotions. I have to keep sacrificing all the time. It's like I am Mother Teresa. You get me, right?" queried Aditya, expressing his married life in the best way he possibly could.

"Sounds like bipolar disorder. You better get it checked," mocked Yuva. "You should have followed my advice to find your best fit. Look at me. I date the best of woman and enjoy my life," he added.

"You date almost every woman you see you horny b*****d," said Mahi.

"Dude, that's because I am a ladies man," retaliated Yuva.

"No you are an aunties man," corrected Aditya hi-fying Mahi who almost fell out of his bed trying to reach Aditya.

Mahi and Aditya laughed like crazy while Yuva was addressing them both in every filthy way possible. No inhibitions whatsoever. It was back to being carefree.

"Aditya, it's difficult. I feel you man. But the most important thing is you need to keep your woman under control. You need to be assertive of your space. The more you care, the more they take advantage. Might be you should take a more hands off, as if I care approach to set things in balance," advised Mahi.

"I feel that urge now and then but I love Aditi too much man. She is my precious. But she has changed a lot since joining her job and now with her promotion and pay hike, it feels like she is in love with her work more than with me" said Aditya.

"What? She earns more than you? Dude are you mad. Let me tell you about a friend of mine, Babu. His wife earned more than him and she used to spend a lot of time at work. He never bothered but used to support her. One fine day, she sends him a divorce notice and only then he comes to know she has been in an affair with her colleague. She didn't respect him because he wasn't her equal and she found a guy who was better than him. Moral of the story: Being economically superior makes one the master, more importantly you the servant," emphatically proclaimed Mahi.

"No, Aditi is not like that but she is getting really busy and we don't spend much time together. That is all what my worry is about. She recently forgot my birthday," revealed Aditya.

"What? She did?" asked Yuva.

"That's how it all starts. First they keep forgetting bits and pieces of you, and one fine day, they forget they even have a husband," said Mahi.

After deep contemplation Aditya told "Do you suggest I should ask her to leave her job? I don't think that's right. Why did she study that hard for and get a degree? To stay at home and be a dish washer? It makes me sound like I am emotionally inferior and insecure. I think I need to respect her individuality."

"Dude, I wonder if she makes all the calls and you just follow it, whose individuality is lost," asked Yuva.

"Eureka enlightenment at last," said Mahi.

"I am not sure. But I think I need to talk to her about it," said Aditya and spoke no further drawn into worrying thoughts by his warring ego and flickering heart.

They had caught up after long. They drank and fooled around. Fed monkeys. Clicked goofy pictures. They enjoyed their sightseeing with some really breathtaking views of nature, while Aditi was still pacifying herself that Aditya will be back and that things would go back to normal soon.

It was almost midnight September 17. Her phone rang. It was Aditya. The mere sight of his face on the screen sent her to dizzy heights. She blushed and took it in a jiffy.

"Hi, Adi. How have you been? Where have you been?"

"Hey, Aditi. I am good. I am at Ooty with Yuva and Mahi. It was an impulsive decision to join them. I wanted to wish you. Have a delightful birthday. God bless."

"I really wish you were here. I have got you some amazing things from Bombay. You will love it."

"Even I really wished you were there on my birthday but most of our birthday wishes never come true, do they?" he spoke curtly and added "Yuva and Mahi are wishing you too." They screamed from behind.

Aditi could feel the pinch of his statement but acknowledged their wishes and thanked them deciding to be silent on the issue.

"Dad and mum said they will meet you tomorrow. If you are busy at work, let them know. They need not take the pains to come all the way," he informed.

Aditi kept quiet. That was her way of dealing with things. She was patient and mature and more understanding of how others felt.

"And one more thing. I have a gift for you in the third row of my bookshelf. Enjoy."

She leapt and swiftly collected it from the book shelf. It was a coupon for a sponsored body care package at a spa.

"Thank you, Adi. That is so sweet of you."

"Sure have fun. I got to go now. You have a good birthday. Will be back in a couple of days. Until then enjoy my absence and me not bugging you," he said and terminated the call.

Aditi wanted to talk more and express herself but this wasn't the time. Two days passed and Aditya dragged his suitcase into the apartment. Again the young chap Krish opened the door for him. Aditya smiled without seeing his eye and walked past him into his bedroom unloading his stuff. Aditi came from the kitchen and hugged him from behind.

"I have missed you so much," she expressed holding onto him.

"Well I have missed you too. How did your week go? The promotion?" he spoke and got out of her arms claiming he was dirty and he had to take a bath.

"It's going to happen I hope," she said and looked at him wondering what was on his mind, whether he had forgiven her.

Aditya gave nothing away and went about picking out his clothes for office and got ready. Aditya was on a call and he shuttled out of the apartment without even wishing her goodbye. Aditi came out of the kitchen and searched and called out for Aditya. Krish informed her that he had left. Aditi felt embarrassed at this situation and Krish had to see all this.

She tried calling Aditya after she reached work but he wasn't responding. I will get back to you in a while was taking a long while now. She got back home early and cooked some really great dinner and waited to surprise

Aditya. But he informed her that he will not be able to come as he was held up with work. There was nothing really at work but he preferred to stay back. He was still wondering how to ask her to quit her job.

Aditi herself was losing it. She has constantly tried to appease Aditya and had apologized so many times now. But his indifference was getting to her. She had to confide in someone and ask for advice. Her colleague Hema was the chosen one. She was a mother of two and had also married twice. She had quite the experience in marital warring. And so Aditi narrated her episode with much reluctance to Hema.

"You poor girl. Why are you so naïve? He is playing with you. He is guilt tripping you. People forget things. I forget my child's birthday sometimes. I forget to feed them sometimes. I forget to collect them back from school sometimes. I forget to give meds to my husband sometimes. It happens. There are two kinds of healing a broken heart. One is you ask for forgiveness and the other one is you get forgiveness," explained Hema as if she was giving a lecture to a rookie.

"No Hema. You don't get it. Aditya is a sweetheart. He is an amazing guy. I just don't know what has got into him."

"It's called chauvinism. He treats you like you are some petty object. He wants to claim that he is the alpha. Trust me, this is just men's tactics to break us into appeasing their ego."

"Okay. But I think I need to talk to him just once and things will be alright," Aditi hoped.

"No, it won't. This is how they are. You better be on your guard," advised Hema.

A day later Aditya was back late yet again after work. He wanted to take a shower as it was a long day at work. Aditi followed in and undressed herself and took a little precaution just in case. Aditya could see her silhouette. That knockout figure he would always compliment her about. He knew his senses were about to be blinded and reason would be much beyond help. He soon ditched the shower and took his towel and walked out. Aditi had lost it.

"What is your problem Aditya? Why do you keep acting like a jerk?"

"Might be because I am one. I am in no mood for this talk," he informed.

"But I plan on sorting this out at this very instance," Aditi insisted. "How could you hold onto something and keep punishing me like this? You haven't even opened the gift I gave you. You are acting so childish. Look Adi, I forgot. It happens. I am human," she added.

"I was hurt. I still am. I hold on to grudges. I don't forgive that easily. I am human too," he responded.

"What has gotten into you? What do you want me to do? Fall on your feet and beg for forgiveness?"

"No just let go off your job. That should do. Everything will fall in place."

"Where is that coming from? I like to be independent. You know me. You even asked me to go for it when I asked whether it was a good idea."

"It sounded like a good idea back then. Not anymore. It has put us through a lot."

"It pays our bills. It helps us afford our luxurious desires."

"So what does my pay do? Look around and jump into our loan repayment? We were happy while in debt. We are out of it. Now the love we had is fading because we don't have time for each other. The best years of your young life is spent on saving for tomorrow. I think just my salary will be enough to afford for both of us."

"This is more about my independence Adi. I like my job. It keeps me from turning into my mother-in-law."

"What do you mean? Why are you pulling my mother into this? Leave it. Do what you like. Just stop bothering me with such unwanted lectures. Let me keep my peace."

Aditya sat on the red bean bag and munched on some Chinese food he had bought for the both of them while Aditi sat hungry and depressed at the kind of predicament she was in. The next day saw Aditi ask Hema for further advice. Hema gave her the I told you so look.

"Men don't change. They just think they are born here to be treated like kings and that we are here to follow their orders and entertain every whim and fancy of theirs. Since your idea of talks have miserably failed, how about some action."

"What do you think I should do?"

"Kindle the jealousy in him. Make him feel like he might lose you. It works on most men. Show your feminine side and be more confident of yourself. That should do. Give him a dose of his own medicine. The notion of losing makes many men learn the value of things they had."

The next day Aditya woke up to a rather dreamy scene. Aditi hadn't dressed this provocatively since their college days. A really low neck, sleeveless red top and a jean that hugged her body and highlighted her curves. It was distracting for any man.

"Don't you have office today? Where are you off to?" asked Aditya.

"I am going to office."

"Like this? Is there some party or something?"

"No. I have a pitch today for a client."

"Did they ask you to dress like this for that? What kind of a company is that?"

"No, it's a fashion company." Aditi thought the advice of Hema had started working. Adi was getting jealous of course but in a very pissed off way.

He giggled and said "Alright. Enjoy."

"What is it, Adi? What is on your mind?" she pondered.

"Nothing, I thought it was a different kind of company. You go ahead."

"What kind of company?" enquired Aditi.

"Nothing. You please go do your thing."

"What kind Aditya?" she stuck out a rude face.

"I thought it was a condom ad. That's about it. Your dress seems a perfect match for that or you could use a bikini. Pitching with that will really get you to a top level in your office. Trust me," he said and walked away.

Aditi was heartbroken at his comment. He hadn't admired her. Things had just gotten worse. Hema had warned of such evasive manoeuvres that men will try to make the woman feel like she was doing something wrong. So she left with the same outfit. It had great response at office. Every guy had his eye out for her. Even married men were passing silly comments at her. She had to bear the cheapness that material men had on their dirty minds.

"So how did it go with your Mr. Jealous?" asked Hema.

"He wasn't jealous at all. He just got wild."

"Jealousy invokes such anger," explained Hema. "You keep being your own person and in due course, it will all be fine."

This kind of dressing had followed the entire week. Aditya was completely annoyed but he just kept his silence and walked in and out knowing things were getting out of control. He dialled Mahi and Yuva for help. The conference call lasted for 10 min. Mahi reiterated his stand on what would happen if he left this unquestioned. Yuva, on the other hand, asked him to act like he doesn't care and instead invoke her jealousy. So the stupidest plan in the history of mankind was hatched.

Aditya had no craving for any woman except Aditi. He dreamt of courting her. He did. He wanted her as his wife. He has that privilege too. Period. There was nothing to ask further. But Yuva asked him to act as if there was this other woman who is interested in Aditya. Yuva's phone number in the contact was to be changed as Preeti, and he also sent the photo of one of his exes to go on display every time the phone rang.

Friday night the plan was put in force. Aditya's mobile was placed next to Aditi. It was around 10 p.m. The phone rang with a different tune. Aditi immediately got up and looked at it. Aditya was coming in from the hall. Preeti looked really pretty on the display. Aditya took the phone and silenced its tune and walked into the next room providing the much needed air of suspicion. Aditi was curious. But she kept a calm exterior without revealing much. Aditya and Yuva giggled at her predicament. This was the plan. Now and then Yuva would call Aditya and it sounded as if there was this Preeti had dialled Aditya the most as per the call log.

Two days later, Aditi couldn't let it go. She stopped Aditya and asked "Who is Preeti?"

"She is a friend of mine. We met at this trip to Ooty. She is friend of Yuva's."

"You never told me, there were women in that trip."

"Well do you tell me everything and she is just a friend. Why do you sound so jealous?"

"A friend who calls a married guy ten times a day and mostly at night. You are acting smart aren't you Adi?" asked Aditi in a rough tone.

"You better mind your tone with me. There is nothing happening like what your imagination is telling you."

The next day morning Mr. Krish was there, and he was complimenting Aditi on her dressing. Aditya could overhear their conversation from the dressing room. Though he felt like he could come out and break Krish's skull open he played it cool. Kokila also time and again warned of Krish who was acting all goody around Aditi. It was mostly fuelling the already raging fire.

Mahi advised Aditya to put a secret camera to trace the behaviour of Krish. He was really getting on Aditya's nerves and Aditi was encouraging it, knowing it was killing Aditya from within. A week later Aditya made his way up to his apartment. He opened the door and saw the most disheartening thing. Krish was almost going to kiss Aditi. She pushed him away and called out to Aditya. Aditya thrashed Krish before he spared his life. Krish ran away.

"Adi thank God. I didn't expect him to behave like this" spoke a panicked Aditi.

"Please Aditi. Stop your drama. I know what's going on between you two. Now it's out in the open. I never thought in my wildest dreams that you would stoop to such a level."

"No Adi, you have mistaken. He forced himself upon me."

"Please I know what I saw. I am happy I came in earlier and not later. Stop your acting. We are done."

He threw the pictures, those beautiful moments and merrier times breaking them in a single blow. The wall stood silent for it couldn't prove her innocence. Aditya was taken by rage and had lost his mind speaking rubbish. Aditi couldn't say further. Trust was broken beyond repair.

Aditya called up Mahi and told him that he was right. "I guess even Aditi can change," he cried. Aditi tried calling Aditya many times but to no avail. He left and thereafter, there was not much joy in Aditi or Aditya's life.

The judge looked at them both and informed them that they would have to go to marriage counselling to try and reconcile to which Aditya opposed. But that was the law and it was the procedure.

"Adi, please believe I have nothing to prove my innocence except my words and my undying love for you. I have reported him to the management and he has been dismissed. Please listen to me," she said tears rolling down her eyes which was a rarity. She never used to cry not even at her own father's death. She stood like a rock and ever since she has been a disbeliever in tears. But she couldn't control them anymore.

"I know I have listened to people I shouldn't have and I did things that were stupid. I am really sorry. Why can't we let this past behind us and start a new life?"

"I am sorry even I did things I should have not. Fought for your integrity before my buddies while I should have trusted them. The only way we can start a new life is by walking away doing our own things," replied Aditya. "If there is a little ounce of love for me, please let me out of this relationship," he added.

Aditi's tears spoke for her but they couldn't move a shattered Aditya. Listening to others without sorting their own mess had got them to losing each other. Aditi consented for divorce after Adi's request. Six months later Aditya reached Aditi's place to take his stuff away from the apartment. Aditi wasn't home. She had gone to the market for shopping. He used the spare key and took all his stuff. He remembered the hidden cam at the top of the book shelf. The doll sat just the same way covered in dirt. It was so unlike Aditi who had an obsessive–compulsive disorder (OCD) for cleanliness.

He took the camera and hesitated to watch any mess that would have been recorded on it. The battery was dead but whatever was recorded was saved. He charged it and decided to watch it now that everything was over. He sank to his knees watching the footage. Aditi had resisted Krish's verbal advances time and again and on that fateful night she had almost taken a knife as Krish was forcing himself on her by which time Aditya entered. After Aditi sent Aditya out she tried to hang herself but she had a change of mind before she went ahead with it.

"Why am I being a coward? I don't want to leave you Adi. I just need to prove my integrity. What got into me?" she said as she sunk into the couch.

She collected the photos strewn all over the place like lifeless memories and hugged them and wept. Aditya time and again used to call Aditi the iron woman who never cried. But that day she did. She did because the only man she gave her heart to didn't trust her anymore.

Her words were recorded loud and clear "I am yours Adi. How could you doubt me? Is that how much you know me? I don't care if the whole world doubted me but how could you?"

Aditya felt a tight rap across his face. All the abuses and words he had thrown at her conduct came right back at him like spears from hell. He could not hide behind the advice of his friend's or even the one inside him who pretended to have unflinching trust of what he had seen with his own eyes. Aditi returned from shopping and was shocked to see Aditya in tears. She sat the groceries on the couch and walked towards him.

"Adi, what is it? What happened?"

Aditya fell on her feet and begged for forgiveness.

A WHITE ROSE FOR THINGS WE LOVED

The white rose garden seemed like a plundered treasure hold. They were bereft of their usual colour and life. Last night, the winds were unforgiving, and the rains had done their part to breathe life into a dying earth. A brief war ensued between the innocent beauty of the myriad roses and the rain drops that seemed like a charging beast. The garden barely survived. To offer life to another, one must sacrifice itself. That's the way of nature. In nature, there is a harmonious arrangement to every life conceived in a pattern much beyond human understanding. The petals lay all around the floor like martyrs of a silent race. No one to place a wreath on them beautiful dead.

Lisa walked into the Little Mother's Old Age Home blushing as broad as daylight. She was back for holidays from her college hostel. She was busy meddling her phone and giggling every time she typed something. Her head was sunk well into the phone that she didn't notice the lack of the old women in her path. No faces to greet or ask her if she was well. It was deserted. It took her a while to finally observe the unnatural silence that welcomed her. Something was not right. She ditched the phone and rushed into the rooms to find out what was going on. No one around. She rushed to the garden as the final destination. The old age home prided itself about the white rose garden. It also featured in a recent news article. It was the chief source of income for the home.

Those who were able to walk picked up the petals and brought them to a corner and those on the wheelchairs had started sorting out the petals that could be salvaged to make a garland of some kind. But most of it were beyond use. The sorting lasted for just a few minutes. The only thing they could make out of it was that the new year was not looking as rosy in terms of paying their bills. They observed a painful silence for a while in memory of the departed souls.

Rani, the most silent and helpful of the lot broke the silence and said "It's like losing our children." Others agreed for they all had taken care of the garden like their own. It helped them cope with the ugly truth of being isolated and deserted by their own kin. It was their only reason to hold on to their faith in loving someone unconditionally. The garden did the duty of their kin. It took care of them for all the care they had bestowed on it.

It was not anymore a commercial relationship. They were not florists. They were caretakers, guardians and in a way each of them was a mother to the garden.

Lisa found them all consoling each other at a corner like the pile of petals on the other end. She was evidently disheartened at the sight of the bare garden that was stripped of its celestial beauty that would infuse love into any heart that walked without it. She ran into the arms of her beloved Shiela, her grandmother, the administrator of the Little Mother's Old Age Home.

"What happened grandma?"

"No one expected the sudden shower my dear. It was around twilight when the skies opened up."

"What are we going to do?"

"We have to do what we always do. Have faith."

The others were slowly getting back into the fold of their usual life still wondering how it will be tomorrow when they look out their windows. Breakfast was to be made ready. Old age had made them depend on medicines. They had to be timely consumed to prolong their existence. In a way the medicines were consuming them. Lisa helped her grandmother to room no. 1, the room of the administrator of the home, where she was an inmate herself.

The phone beeps had increased in its constancy mimicking a ticking time bomb.

"What is it? Check the alarm," informed Shiela.

"It's my phone. They are notification sounds."

"The sounds are quite in tune with an annoying alarm, aren't they?" asked Shiela.

Lisa controlled her impulses to retaliate and defend the best of technological advancements and promptly agreed to change the ringtone given the loss which had accrued to them. Lisa went back into her phone more merrier with her eyes widening unavailable for a conversation as Shiela started a mutual conversation that ended up a monologue.

"You know, you better tell him soon that you like him or you gonna get fat after eating ice creams to keep your depression away," Shiela abruptly suggested.

"Uh, huh…hmmmm, okay," responded Lisa.

A little while later, the words struck Lisa.

"What granny?"

"The fellow you are texting seems like he has secretly entered your heart. I have felt it for sometime now."

"No, no, he is just a friend."

"You keep telling that to yourself and someday soon you will certainly be right. He will only be your friend and you will be regretting it."

"Nonsense. It's not 1950s grandma. We speak our hearts and are open about what we want."

"As much as I gather with my limited knowhow of this generation, you are more confused about love and friendship than we were. It has become synonymous at your age just like the fallacy of interchangeably using truth and opinion in this generation."

"Granny, worry not. I don't like him like that. He is a very nice guy. I like his company. That's all."

"That is the start of all, my dear."

"Granny, please leave this discussion. I am not here to debate. What are we going to do about the garden?"

"We have to restart. Plant fresh roots and take more precautions."

"But where is the money for all this? Wish dad and mum were alive. They would have done something."

"They already did the best thing they could do for us," Shiela said placing her hand on Lisa.

"Stop being emotional, granny. What are we going to do?"

A loud noise erupted in the hallway. Mrs. Nandini had fallen unconscious on the floor. She used to be a psychiatrist at the Government Hospital. All new comers had a tough time before they could settle in. They had no immunity towards suddenly becoming unwanted. Even a person who had specialized in human emotions was no exception to such an emotional shock. Old and weak hands that were around still preserved the strength of humanity and empathy to lift her pale and thin figure.

Mr. Rohit, the doctor who was kind enough to provide medical help free of cost, was summoned at once. He lived right at the end of the street. He was still gearing up for the day but he happily obliged and rushed down in his pyjamas to keep the old age home in surplus of a psychiatrist. The needle had pushed some much needed nerve strengthening concoction, and she was at rest in her bed still living her troubles at some part of her mind with her eyes closed.

"Thank you so much doctor. We are sorry for disturbing you at this early hour. You have been really kind and we keep asking much of you," said Shiela with her hands doing the namskar.

"Why do you do this Ma? I have been forever in your debt. Dad always spoke high of you and said he owed his life to you and without him I would have been a nobody."

"Lisa go and get a cup of coffee for the doctor," said Shiela.

"No. Thank you Ma. I have a long day ahead of me. I promised my wife I will be back to have her version of the coffee," Rohit sheepishly smiled.

"She will be waiting," Rohit excused himself.

"You make a fine husband. It's not just coffee. It's her love too," Shiela said in an advisory tone.

"I know. I know. I certainly hope there is more to her coffee than what I can taste," Rohit laughed light heartedly and bid farewell jogging his way back with his doctor kit.

Lisa had a tough time comprehending the efficacy of a prayer meet being arranged whenever someone went sick or seriously sick (code word for nearing the end). It almost never helped them as eventually nature took over and the other members of the home bid their goodbyes to the parting soul. It was Lisa's duty to get everyone on time to gather and lead them in prayer.

"Now, I have to be the priestess yet again. I am doing this almost every alternate day of every week. I better start continuing with a sermon next time. I hope God takes into account all this and scores me to heaven when he tallies my account," she mumbled as she crashed her mobile into the white fluffy pillow.

"Stop your mumbling. You are providing hope and that's the most noble thing to do in all the world. Remember this, for those who can't spend even nominally to restore their failing health a prayer is the most consoling pill and a miracle is their only hope," reprimanded Shiela.

The prayer was usually done the Christian way. Lisa subscribed to it. That was the material available to her on the net. It was simple. She liked it. Simple words, not many polysyllabic ones and an amen at the end. Others joined her without imposing their own religious customs and sincerely prayed to alleviate their comrade from her suffering. But they all knew that they weren't far behind from a prayer meet being conducted for them.

The prayer meet was kept short. It was a Saturday. Mostly, it involved the inmates wishing the person a lot of good health which never reached them on time. But the practice had made them care for one another. It helped in a subconscious way. This was followed by an organic breakfast.

Lisa rushed into Shiela's room to pick her phone similar to anyone who would embrace their long lost lover. Only a brief half an hour, they had parted. There had been an incessant flow of messages. Some from her friends, some from random groups she was recruited to without her consent yet she chose to stay within keeping in mind social decorum and some stupid advertisements that were meant mostly for men with bald heads. But she chose very carefully to entertain that friendly companion she referred to as "just a friend." Her close friends had to wait. "Just a friend" guy became important enough that his confession that he had no clue why he likes texting her became a clutching point of discussion. An inference into this universal delusion or psychological quirk that we all go through trumps every other intellectual debate and finds more takers. Even after centuries of immense evolutionary contemplation flirting still remains the most inexhaustible source of sweet somethings.

Shiela was already making calls to the nearby florists informing that the stock of roses the home had undertaken to provide will not reach them due to the heavy rains. She was delegating tasks to her fellow members to start the repair works in the garden. As things were, the shortage of funds was the most pressing matter. But whatever that could manually be done was done. The soil was made suitable again despite the dark clouds threatening to pour down. Shiela remarked "It's our fortune. Go ahead. What is fortune but an everlasting battle between effort and circumstance."

The watchman and his sons helped in putting up a temporary shamyana to protect whatever was left of the fallen roses. They needed to get bare roots of roses to plant. Shiela had weathered enough of monsoon woes.

She wanted to put into action her glasshouse plan for the garden. Lisa took Shiela to the cooperative bank. Shiela had kept aside some gold ornaments for Lisa's education and future. She decided to pledge them and fund the glasshouse and save the home left with no other choice. The locker had last been opened at the time Lisa's parents expired. The medical expenses had eaten a chunk of the gold but was not enough to seal the deal with fate. Shiela had carefully saved much of the money earned by her husband who was an agriculturalist by profession. Those days, the pulses and cereals were healthier and the nature believed in the hard labour of man, and it kept its promise. But slowly the greed of man consumed him and nature withdrew its benevolence. She lived frugally and spent only on the essentials of life. That austere living benefitted her now.

The loan was procured within a fortnight, and work was underway with a blueprint drawn to construct the glasshouse. The threatening skies had withdrawn, and there was the shimmer of hope running through those old weakened souls that held onto dear life passing through every day as if it were their last.

Now came the need to procure bare roots for planting. The space in the garden upon installation was planned in such a way to provide for more variety of roses. The labour charges and material costs had exceeded the value of loan that the remaining quantum of gold could facilitate. They had exhausted their economic resources. All loans had been borrowed. Anything more just meant it was charity, and no way of repaying was even remotely possible. But Shiela bore a smile and walked with the help of Lisa once more to the locker at the bank. An old cloth bag that had been unearthed from under the ground was kept safe in a polythene bag. It was heavy and dirty.

"What is it granny?" asked Lisa.

"The last remaining symbol of my love," she answered with tears gripping her eyes.

Lisa hugged and consoled her grandmother.

"Grandpa is always with us. I know you miss him."

Shiela wiped her eyes and took out a necklace that bore diamonds which was an antique worth a few lakhs.

"Wow. How was grandpa able to afford such a pricey thing?" enquired Lisa.

Shiela kept quite. She was deep with her memories, and Lisa did not insist further on her answering.

There was a deep contemplation that Shiela was engaged in. She refused to entertain anyone at her room that evening, even Lisa. A week passed and things were returning at a faster pace in favour of the home. Shiela had requested Lisa not to inform anyone of how the additional sum of money was made ready. It was a charitable gesture by some big hearted people was her answer. Lisa followed suit.

February 14 had come to pass. Lisa returned early. Shiela could recognize the tone in her voice was screaming to let out some emotional clutter. But Shiela politely waited for Lisa to start the conversation. Lisa spoke less and went to bed without much inclination towards dinner. The next day, Shiela made her some tea and began a conversation.

"What is it Lisa? You have been away from your phone lately?"

"It is nothing granny."

"So, it has nothing to do with you crying last night?"

"You were awake?"

"When my darling granddaughter is in tears, how can I get a peaceful sleep? It's that guy, isn't it?"

"Yes, granny. You were right. He is my friend now and only my friend."

"Why didn't you tell him, my dear?"

"The guy has to approach and ask me grandma and not the other way around. Moreover, he likes my friend Rekha."

"You mean he has asked your friend Rekha?"

"Yes. He did. He knows nothing about her. She is all drama."

"That settles it anyway. He likes her. What are you worried about then?"

"I thought he would ask me. I was so foolish. I have embarrassed myself," cried Lisa.

"Dear Lisa, what has got into you? He was never meant for you."

"You don't understand grandma. I have been friendzoned."

"What is that? Is that a bad thing?" asked Shiela.

"Arghhh…you don't know how these things hurt. I even confessed to my close friends that I like him. Let's not speak about this and waste another day. I want to get over him," Lisa said applying wet tissues on her sleep deprived eyes.

"You poor girl. What made you believe he liked you?"

"We had something granny. I can tell you he liked me. I didn't feel like that with anybody else."

"Well, here is the thing Lisa. I think he was just fooling around."

"No granny. He is not that kind of a guy. I know him."

"You poor thing. Then go and tell him you like him. I think waiting for the guy to ask is stupid."

"What are you saying granny? He is a very close friend. He has texted me last night and even this morning and I haven't responded. I can't at least for now. He likes Rekha. Let's go get that ice cream you were talking about. The guy needs to ask. That is the way the world works. That's how it is done."

"How could you ever be my granddaughter?"

"What? Why would say something like that when I am already hurt?"

"For your information I told the man I loved that I liked him and I did it first. Sure he was taken aback. But he sure as hell knew I was a romantic."

"What you told grandpa first?"

"No. Not your grandfather. But the man I fell in love with."

"What? You loved someone else? Then why did you marry grandpa?"

Shiela started to share her story that had happened five decades earlier.

"That was us. A little shy and very much tangled in love," Shiela revealed a black and white photo of a young man and herself from within one of her sarees in her cupboard. She never spoke to anyone of his identity. She had kept it with her for long, and she would touch and embrace it every time she missed the one man she truly loved. The picture was almost losing all signs of life. It was nearing a white empty smudge of memory. The couple in the picture were trying their best to contain themselves from laughing but they held each other, the woman her hands around his neck and the man with his arms tied around her hips uncomfortably. The next move was the kiss.

"To add embarrassment, the kiss unfortunately landed on my nose. A memory for a lifetime. I still remember the scent on him, the wet innocence of a spontaneous kiss. Five decades ago, I met the love of my life. He was an orphan much disliked by a society lost in its rigid ways of judging innocent souls by their birth. Everything had an order but the order was not right. Not even close to right. Something was dearly wrong, but even money back then was unable to undo many things. Communal feelings took precedence over humans and least of all human emotions. Men were respected by their birth into nobility as opposed to their deeds. A man of a higher caste was declared a saint, and that he was incapable of sins. A sense of belonging to an elite class made few men and women the epitome of arrogance. My father was one such man, a slave to irrational sentiments of his ancestors. I belonged to an elite class by default. I was no good in defending my sense of belonging. To be honest, I never had one. I belonged with him that is all I knew then.

My love was a free soul. We met at my private tutor's home. He worked as his assistant. I remember the day we first met each other. He wouldn't raise his eyes to see me.

That was the norm established by the high caste of my village. Neither did I initially. But he was a smart looking guy my intermittent glances around my tutor's home had recorded.

Mr. Love was a thin frame and a dark skinned man who had nothing short of a rockstar voice. It had a command and polish to it. But unfortunately, he wasn't born into a commanding clan. The private tutor Mr. Swami had a kind heart, a good social status and two cows he revered much more than anything in this world, his wife included.

"I love these cows. I wanted to be an agriculturalist. But my community made me a man of faith and a teacher. Even the nobility of my profession has never been enough to undo the regret of not following my heart. Thankfully, these cows are the closest I could get to living my dream," he recollected his anguish frequently.

There in the distance, the cow shed had found a new teacher. It was my man using his flawless pronunciations to educate hungry cows who were feeding on a pile of greens about the ill effects of a dry spell of monsoon. Accidently, I slipped on the stairs completely engrossed in the conversations he was having with the cows. A loud thud had caught his attention. He rushed to me at once and helped me rise up. Nothing stopped him, not even the reminder that he belonged to a lesser caste.

"I am sorry. I didn't mean to touch you intentionally. But you had been hurt. I couldn't help but help you. Sorry. What am I saying? Please forgive me."

Mr. Swami and his wife rushed to the scene and enquired of my wellness. I was careful not to credit my man for it. Even touching a woman of a higher caste by a man belonging to a lower caste was met with severe punishments in the panchayat run by men of elite class.

He had no ego to hold onto. The society made sure of that. But he had a beautiful heart and anyone who met him more than once could see it. I had the opportunity of seeing it every day. I even felt it. He had a quick grasp of things. Mr. Swami always had a soft corner for him and taught him basic maths and some slokas once in a while. We had an awful silence, when we met during the classes.

"Mrs. Swami, please bring us something to drink," yelled Mr. Swami to his partially deaf wife time and again.

The scream was never for Mrs. Swami. It was for him. He would bring two full glasses of buttermilk very carefully and would place it on the wooden plank before Mr. Swami and sit beside him listening to the class. He would glance at me from the corner of his eye now and then. I noticed it. He noticed that I noticed it but still continued. A smile would uncomfortably erupt occasionally and die down before Mr. or Mrs. Swami came. The first most daring thing he did.

A year had passed, and I knew it was more the prospect of meeting him that made me go to class than the actual process of assimilating knowledge. He grew a kind fondness to me. A good friendship despite the barrier of silence had grown deep. Post-independence, there was still a lingering sway of silent crimes perpetrated by our own people against each other in the name of communal hierarchy.

A few days after the new year of 1952, I could no longer see the face of that man I had befriended. I could only realize and accompany the vacuum he had left behind. I couldn't initiate a conversation with Mr. Swami about his absence or that would raise questions I was in no position to answer. My eyes would fervently search day after day if there were any traces of him. This time of separation made me understand that deep within me, there was this nameless feeling that was near to invincible, something my mind even after finding great reason could not convince. Something more profound than reason had come over me, and it swept me off like a mere particle of dust that was blown away by a heavy gush of unapologetic wind. There was still no hope of seeing him but the memories of those pleasant encounters would not rest. They had found a life of their own within me that I had nurtured without my knowledge. The enlightenment of being in love is difficult to perceive, much more difficult to understand and impossible to let go.

Six months had gone by and I was near to leaving Mr. Swami's home tuition dejected and unable to resolve my feelings for him when Mr. Swami received a telegram intimating his arrival. Mr. Swami I could say was the most relieved man on earth after hearing the news. His man Friday was back. I couldn't control my happiness either but I put up a calm exterior while my heart was pounding much to the pace of a rabbits run. That night was the most memorable of all. I couldn't sleep. I wore a dumb grin all over my face. My mom almost came to the conclusion that someone had used black magic on me. I had made up my mind to continue at Mr. Swami's. I had gone through the last 6 months with an undecided future about him but waiting just another week was when time moved slowest for me. The only thing that ran on my mind was whether he would have housed similar feelings for me. Time is an adversary in love. It runs mercilessly fast. It runs painfully slow.

The week had passed, and he was in town but I had not met him yet. Mrs. Swami was animatedly talking to someone by the kitchen. I walked in hoping to meet him but Mr. Swami was already there seated on his elevated mat. A new lady placed the buttermilk. Finally my man entered with a more refined dressing and a more rounded physique. But his innocence was not lost. I glanced hoping he would smile back but that never happened. He rushed back to the cow shed.

"Look at the shyness of a newlywed," Mr. Swami conveyed the shattering news. He had been married. The new bearer of the buttermilk was the lucky lady. I could no longer stay around and feign any interest in learning things that mattered to the world. The one thing that mattered to me was no more mine. I could understand that feeling of becoming numb. I could not feel anything or speak to anyone of how I felt. I was helpless and I could no longer take it. I wanted to know if I ever meant something to him.

A week later I resumed class only to find out whether he ever liked me the way I liked him or felt about him. In the break time, I walked right to the cow shed. He stood feeding the cows and brushing their bodies. Before I could start, he spoke much to my amusement.

"What brings you here madam? May I help you?"

"What happened? Why did you marry?" I started.

"What are you talking about?" he retaliated.

"I have been waiting for a little over 6 months to tell you how much I like you."

He stood unaffected by what he had heard and went on giving water to a belching cow. Time was running out and I had to get back. But I needed an answer. I had got out what was haunting me for the last 6 months. So I stood. His wife came and wished me. I smiled back. With every word of kindness, he showered to his wife I was burning within. Call it jealousy or anything but that was how I felt. I felt let down. I felt unwanted. A mix of many unpleasant emotions. He waited until his wife left.

"I wish I could tell you I never felt that way about you. But I would be lying. I couldn't contain myself a few months back. I would have almost blurted it out. Mr. Swami put some sense into me. He reminded me what it would mean to go against the social will. I didn't know how you felt. I couldn't gather the guts to ask. Even then in all honesty the match was uneven. I could never expect to marry someone like you. You are a flawless woman, and if I ever dreamt of even asking your hand in marriage, the world would only call me a fool. We both have heard stories of uneven matches at Mr. Swami's teachings but they are heroic and practical as far as stories go. I don't deserve you. I belong with the cows and other common things."

"But you never asked me. How could you think that I wouldn't like you?"

"There was no way of knowing. If I did ask and should you reject I shall forever live with a pain much beyond any expression. The society wouldn't approve anyway. I could not survive causing pain to myself or to you. Love happens and it shall pass too."

"I still love you and nothing will change that," I said and turned back to the class.

He stood there shocked at my way of expression and wanted to convince me that the same could never happen henceforth. He was right. I knew well within that there was nothing I could do. I felt somewhat happy for the lucky woman. She was contented, caring and most important of all belonged to a lower community. How I wished I could shed my community and become his lover. But as things were, I was no home wrecker. I respected her for who she was. She was a good wife. He looked happy. Their family was worth the burying of my unfinished love.

Shiela now with her shaking hands reached the photo and held it once again close to her heart. Lisa had forgotten her debacle. She never knew this. No one knew this.

"Granny, it's alright."

"Lisa dear I am sure of this one thing. It pains even after all these years to have never been able to marry the man you loved."

Lisa hugged her grandma tight. Two women who dearly missed their men were in need of a hug more than tissues. Lisa wiped her tears and understood the many sensitive layers that a woman would evolve into. She never knew this side of her grandma.

"How come you never told me all this while? Did dad know about this?"

"No. Even you would not have if not for me being sorely reminded after pledging the last symbol of my love."

"So tell me how did this photo happen then?"

Three years had passed and I had been rejecting every proposal my parents had brought for me. My parents were losing hope and were losing face before an intrusive social set up. They were fighting hard to defend stories of an illusory terminal illness I was suffering from, and some said I had a mental problem. But only I knew it was love and I would be unable to love any other man ever so truly that I never consented to it.

I was no more going to Mr. Swami's private classes. I kept away. I heard the news that the man I still love had gone to his wife's village and settled back there. Somehow I had been too sure he was for me. The feelings I had developed would not listen to moral qualms of the shame of wandering behind a married man. The failing health of mom had got the better of a serious lack of marital interest. It became an implied duty to appease the dying soul of my mother. So I consented to an arrangement. My family called it a wedding.

Two untimely deaths had brought my love back to me. My mom died right after my engagement. The poor soul couldn't see her child marry a man of such despicable qualities. The customs of that time dictated that no auspicious function would take place for the next one year. The bridegroom was a wealthy and powerful man born into the same community as I, but had poor care for manners. The irony was he was named Ramakrishnan. A complete insult to mythical sentiments. He was no Ram or Krishna. His lust had made more unspeakable stories. He was an object to detest. The only thing my father was sure about was the social rank and the abounding pomp and wealth that came along with his impeccable notoriety record.

The second death was that of the wife of the man I loved. She died while giving birth to their child. He stayed there for 7 months wrestling with memories of his good wife. Later, he sold all his lands there and got back here wanting to start a new life with his child here. I heard news of his arrival because his newfound wealth had irked the people of an elite class. I overheard my father plotting with other men of our community to cut him to size and show him his place. I could not be a bystander. I had to warn him. I went to the house he had hired for temporary stay.

I left my house informing I was out to get some utensils at the country market fair. I made sure I was not being followed. The bungalow was a guest house for people who could afford it. To see the man I loved grow into wealth was a joy that I had to contain deep within. The cry of a child welcomed me as it lay there on the floor wrapped in soft silk. I held the little one up and somehow it calmed the little one to merely hold my fingers and fall into a dreamy sleep. A man from the kitchen arrived with a small spoon and sweetened milk. The infinite happiness that had caught hold of me had caught hold of him too I could sense. He showed me to a chair and stood, while I rested with a beautiful baby on my lap.

"Let me take him," he offered.

"Let me at least keep him for a while," I requested.

"How are you, Shiela?"

I looked at him and nodded without conveying my true emotions.

"I am sorry for your loss. She was a kind and noble woman to see," I complimented his wife.

He spoke not. His tears had the job done for him.

"What would you like to have?"

"No don't trouble yourself with being courteous. You will not be able to give what I need."

An awful silence and an ill-timed smile erupted conveying my desire to accompany him again if he would have me. The hints had been dropped. He understood them well but held back his answer.

"I came here to warn you. My elders and other men from the panchayat don't like you or your wealth. They don't mean well. Please be safe. Please leave."

"Why are you telling me this? You are asking me to leave the only place I had spent a large part of my life."

"You protect the things you love. You wouldn't want them to be harmed in any way. That is why. I wish you live longer and happier though I will miss what time had returned to me."

I had started to tear apart and I was fighting my tears back.

"Will you come along if I leave?" he said with his eyes looking into mine and his hand wiping my tears.

I could only cry further then. He had answered me.

"Shall we leave right away," I enquired bowing down to kiss the baby.

"Not right away," he laughed with a twinkle in his eyes.

It was the season of love in my life I had believed as things were falling into place yet again.

The optimist in him believed that men like my father could be changed. That was where he had erred.

I snuck out for more country market fair purchases now and then spending time with him, knowing him, loving him more and almost believing we would soon be together as husband and wife. A week later, I went to the guest house where he stayed. I was informed he no longer stayed there and that he had checked out 2 days back. I was given a letter that bore my name on it.

"Meet me at Mr. Swami's," it read.

I rushed to Mr. Swami's house where Mr. Swami welcomed me.

"He has told me everything. I think you should leave immediately with him. But he would not listen to me. I am sure your father will see you and him dead before consenting to your union," said Mr. Swami.

I looked at him concerned at what would be our fate. Mrs. Swami who came to know about us had gone behind our back and quietly informed Ramakrishnan whom she owed money.

The cow shed had somehow become a nostalgic remembrance of how I met the man I loved. I saw him holding the baby and feeding the cows with the same care and concern.

"Why did you come to Mr. Swami?"

"I couldn't afford the guest house anymore."

"Why what happened?"

"I spent my money."

"On what did you spend your money?"

"You like me even without my wealth, right?"

"I do. Now answer my question," I said.

He handed the baby to me and took out that beautiful thing that we pledged. It was his gift to me.

"I spent my money on this. I also purchased a piece of land that we will cultivate in the Palki town."

I was still admiring the beautiful piece of jewellery that was a symbol of our love. It was crafted to perfection and as he placed it on my neck I leapt forward and kissed him in the cheek. He stood there turning red and was knocked completely out of his senses as he didn't expect such a gesture from me.

Mr. Swami was gifted a camera by him and Mr. Swami offered to take a picture of us together. That is the one I have been guarding as a treasure for this long. I could only think that he mustered the courage to kiss me after what I had done to him. I must have passed on some courage to him. Mr. Swami was certainly shocked. We had planned to leave our village two days later. As I left that eve, he gave me a white rose. I placed it on my head as a mark of respect and walked back to my house.

Ramakrishnan was killed two days later on the night when we were to leave. Killed by the man I loved to save my integrity. But I knew he had a child to take care and without him, it would be orphaned. So I had to let go of him. I sent him away with his child. I stayed back took the blame for it, if they knew it was him they wouldn't leave him alive.

"A white rose for the things we love but can never have," he finally said and placed a white rose that was partially soaked in the blood of a scoundrel in my hands. I saw a crying baby and a mourning lover pass by me. The man I loved saved me and I saved him in return well aware that what we had done would part us for the rest of our lives.

Years passed and I married a man who was a choice of my father. I respected him and stayed loyal to him but I could never live with the man I fell in love with and that would forever stay a regret. I would have wished life was the way I liked, and I had hoped for more than once that fate would deal the cards in my favour. But it was not so kind."

"Now, Lisa my dear, it is not what you feel for someone that makes you vulnerable. It shows the incredible potential of the bond you may share if both of you had mutual feelings and chose to believe in it. You must at all cost speak your heart for love may be lost but the feelings that you experienced will never shy away. It will become a part of you making you heartbroken and even more sceptical of love. The world will have a million ways of doing things. Wait for love. Not the confession of it. Go for it. Tell him how you feel and give him a white rose from our garden."

"Granny, did you see him again? Who is he?"

"I did. But then I was married and had a son. I had made certain compromises and I chose to live with it. I wish you knew him as the man who I dearly love to this day."

The next day Lisa came back all excited. She had done what her granny asked her to. It turned out that Rekha said no.

"So you are telling me fate dealt you a favourable card," Shiela said.

"Yes, granny. I am so happy. Everything is sorted out. Our home is safe. The garden is looking beautiful again. There has been no incident of prayer meets for over 2 weeks now. There is a good chance 'only my friend' guy will be more than my friend."

Mr. Rohit had come back the next day for a regular check-up and sat down for tea with Shiela and Lisa.

"How is your wife Rohit?" enquired Shiela.

"She is worried about my earning capacity. She worries I don't earn enough for my profession. I prefer giving medical aid to the needy free of cost. But she doesn't understand."

"You get that from your father. He was a very kind and noble man as I remember him. How is your son?"

"It's funny you should ask about my son. A curious thing happened a week ago. He came back dejected that his valentine had rejected him. Two days back he comes with the happiest face I have seen him with. He had a white rose in his hand, and he said he has found his soulmate. Adolescents these days are so confused and naïve."

Shiela looked at Lisa. Lisa grinned embarrassed by the revelation.

"The more curious thing is he said the exact same thing my father used to tell me. A white rose for the things we love but can never have."

Lisa looked at Shiela. Shiela smiled back.

HOW THEY MET EACH OTHER

"He likes Sunny Leone. His views on religion are Gods must be crazy. He listens to jazz, and his pictures reveal he is a poser mostly with women and his friends list have men and women in a ratio of 1:3, respectively," listed the nerdish looking Radha Rammohan adjusting her glasses and twisting her lips and evenly spreading a good quantity of lip moisturiser that had stuck to her finger.

"Well so what? All of us have our musings. He is a really sensitive person within I am told. Just meet him once Rad," requested Janaki still adjusting the frills of her best friend's saree.

"She looks a little dark. But she has got sharp facial features and she looks hot minus her colour. But that's not what I am after. I am so not into these feminist extremist type of women who border on insanity after Kavya. Her opinions are so conservative and founded on ancient beliefs that are so irrelevant today. She follows leaders and Nobel Prize winners on twitter. Her favourite books include Das Kapital, Mein Kampf and The Man Unknown. What am I gonna date? A general knowledge book? or worse a philosophy book. Does she even belong to this century? I need someone who can process me with a heart and not her mind. Most intellectual beings lack heart da. Show me someone else," said Krishna Subramanian.

"Well, I know Kavya was a little annoying," started Raghav.

"A little? A little? Dude she is the source code for annoying," corrected an evidently pissed Krishna.

"Alright. But that doesn't mean every woman is going to be like her."

"Yes. I made a wild choice when I chose her and I couldn't really live up to her expectations. But you know there is something called probability that runs on the principle of aggregating experiences and predicting a future event. One of the most underutilized and wilfully ignored prudency tool of mankind. I can sense her to belong there with Kavya at the Hall of Super nutcases."

"Why don't you just give it a chance? You never know she might just be the one."

"Sorry da. I am not for it. Now, please let me be off on my blind date. How do I look?"

"You look like a cool guy who has no clue his fly is open," giggled Raghav.

Krishna fixed his dress and bid goodbye to a disappointed Raghav. Janaki and Raghav were in a relationship. They met at a common friend's birthday party. It was love at first sight. They felt connected and one thing led to another. Everything was well, and they were getting to know about each other's family and friends. That is when they spoke about Krishna who had a recent break up that was devastating and Radha, an equally lonely person who feared getting into a relationship after her one-sided love for a close friend. They decided to talk them into seeing each other. It had now proved futile.

The night was still young, and people were busy wearing masquerades, getting into the The Love Story Blind date event. It was a special one. No one knew the theme was going to be literally incorporated. There were totally 20 pairs. There were all kinds of romantics there.

The ones who were single looking out for a relationship, the ones who were wanting out of a relationship, then those who were in love with the idea of a blind date, then those who came confidently with the sole idea of proposing and marrying the one they meet there since their stars had aligned in such a lucky manner and there were those who were divorced wanting to find new love.

Love has many forms, most of it quite exquisitely challenging human perception. The most central of our beliefs are attached to the ability of man to understand the intricacies of the why, what, where, who and when of things. The only exception being love. No one knows when, who, where and most importantly the why. The only reaction after that is what? Though mostly it comes as a reaction that expresses shock or disbelief. What was I doing? and what was I thinking? kind of thing.

"What are you saying?" asked a disappointed Janaki as Raghav revealed the decision of Krishna.

"Did Radha accept?" queried Raghav.

"No, she is half in and half out as always. Mostly confused by his Facebook (FB) account's 'About you' column."

"What's wrong with that? He is a really nice guy Janu."

"Yes, I know that but his FB account doesn't speak high of him." , replied Janaki.

"What? In what way?"

"Radha feels he is more like a cynical and flamboyant type who can't be real. He likes Sunny Leone. That was one of her grievances. Speaking of which even you seem to like her on your account, and there are a dozen other models whom I have never seen who mostly seem to think they are still babies in terms of their dressing."

"What is wrong with Radha? Who doesn't like Sunny? And most importantly half the people on FB like pages because their friends recommend it. They don't have the bloody time to find whether it's authentic or if it's even something they like. No one goes to the pages, and someday some random image is posted from that page and even then one doesn't remember to have liked that page. It's like having a hangover. No one remembers a thing. I can't remember my friend's birthday. It's on FB. It's a convenience that supports the fallacy of a poor memory. She shouldn't go making choices based on that."

"What is my favourite colour? No wait. When is my birthday Raghav?"

"Umm...sometime in November 20's."

"Oh, I see. Is that how much you remember? When was the day when we first met?"

"See, I told you I am bad at dates. We met at Shashank's birthday party. Anyway, why are we analyzing our relationship?"

"You don't seem to recall the most significant date of our lives. That's annoying."

"Well, since you seem to know, tell me when my birthday is."

"August 21, 1991. And next year you will be 25, so I am planning on getting you 25 gifts."

"You must have seen on FB since we are at it."

"We met on September 15 at 8:30 p.m. You wore a brown shirt and a black jean."

Raghav said no more and was cursing the maker for creating him with such poor memory.

"Alright, I am sorry Janu. This is me. I am not perfect but I loved you from the moment we met."

"There is always a start for everything. Might be it's time you get perfect," came the reply.

Meanwhile, there was a kind of heavy breathing that comes with anxiety and uncertainty, and the event witnessed some tripping and tumbling at The Love Story Blind date. The lights were off. That's how they will stay announced the organizers. Today, we will identify how compatible you and your assigned partner will be. The true appearance of compatibility is best known when you don't judge your partner for the very first time based on looks. Appearance should at no opportunity compensate for compatibility. The lady participants were seated at their assigned tables. The men slowly moved towards their assigned table numbers that briefly glowed for a minute by which time they had to reach their tables. There was a lot of chatter and restless air in the hall. Krishna had a little tumble only to be held by his pair. He fell right on her feet.

"Why so soon?" she said with a sparkle and childish playfulness in her voice.

Krishna was a little shaken at his misfortune but however he conveyed his thanks for her help still admiring that silky voice.

She said politely "Shall I let you in on a little secret?"

"What is it Miss. 8?" They were instructed not to disclose their true identity, and address each other by their assigned numbers. Additionally, they were also instructed not to disclose any personal details and to only play by the instructions of the organizers and to abide by the rules. They had microphones under each table and violators will be sent out they announced.

"Mr. 8, I too had a tumble but no one knows about it except you. Hope you don't tell anyone"

"I am sure no one will believe me given that your voice will keep them mesmerized and oblivious to anything others say."

"I am blushing and it's my duty to tell you since you can't see in all this darkness. You are a sweet talker Mr. 8."

They were getting along fine until the organizers started the event. "Since we gather that everyone has found a table, let's start," blared the loudspeaker.

"Okay," they all cheered and so it began. The first instruction was to learn about each other's exes.

Why they fell in love with them and why they broke up and they were instructed to narrate it as a story.

The first stage was to last for 15 min.

Krishna started the story with a "Ladies first."

"He is the only guy who I ever fell in love with and he liked me not for my looks. It's like he could see right through all my exterior facades. I feel like I have no defence against him. He is not the most good-looking but his smile, his talk, his walk, his eyes and his manners reflect an aura that is hard to resist for any woman. He is that guy who does not take pride in his intelligence though everyone around him compliments time and again about it. He does not act smart with me and treats me like I know better. He is the only guy who treats me like I matter the most to him. He is the guy who has never hesitated to tell me when I am wrong, and something within me bells my rebellious nature and tells me I have to listen to him. To him, I confess to everything. He is the only guy who knows why I cry and makes sure that it never happens and if it does, he makes sure he does something stupid to embarrass himself to see a smile on my face. He is the only guy who listens patiently to me scold him and actually says it sounds like a poem though the neighbour lady looks at me with contempt. He knows my thoughts even before I do, and some odd feeling tells me that in him is should trust and only him. His kiss is the only thing I would want to wear on my lips. He respects me with all my flaws. He is the one who cooks with me and says it's delicious even though the cat wouldn't have it. He is the only guy that I want to talk to if it were my last. And what's more curious is I feel he is mine."

"Wow. Do such guys exist? Your ex seems like he is right out of a fairy tale and I can with much certainty tell you are not over him."

"I will never be. My first love. I learnt to love for the first time. It's special."

"Why did you break up then?"

"I am not sure. Tell me your story now," she divulged from the question and egged on Krishna. Deep within Krishna knew Ms. 8 was single, and she had never been in a relationship and her narration was her expectation of a promising partner. But he felt he wanted to stick around and listen to her tale. It was intense and lovely. So, he slowly started.

"She was pretty, decent and much beyond my dreams. She was a unusually strong willed woman. She could war a thousand men and never lose. She never wanted to and I made sure she didn't at least with me. She was adamant about petty things. She had a way of putting things in perspective. She was plain spoken but in love, words need to be a little on the kinder side. It is very easy to feel like everything is lost when your love doesn't respond to you anymore in a way you had both connected before. I was a lucky guy I used to think earlier. I was the envy of my friends for courting her. She was more refined and mature, and I looked like an imbecile before her. I never bothered about it earlier but somewhere down the lane, I felt I was taken for granted.

She was a sweetheart for the initial part but later she started to take on the role of a military general. I lost my space and I felt like I had been possessed by her living self. I had to follow her words and I felt no equal in the relationship. She had taken to drinking and smoking. I disliked it. Though it might sound unbelievable and even shameful as it is made up to be I am proud to announce myself as a teetotaller. In our love story, everything was about her and I featured in it now and then like the conjunction that joined two sentences which were about her. She was a complex being much beyond my understanding.

I respected her feminist ideologies but it was when she started to make me feel like a joke I wanted to get out of it. So I left realizing I was never meant for her. I am wild and annoyed at myself for choosing her and breaking her heart in the bargain. I think it was mostly my fault to have gotten her into something I didn't know to handle. She deserved a better man with a stronger persona, intelligence and modern ideologies. I couldn't bear her drink. But who doesn't these days. I asked her to wear clothes that looked pretty on her. But she liked it being sexy. I think I liked her initially because she looked sexy but later it dawned on me that I am old school. She would have looked awesome in a saree. She never wore it for me even when I requested her to. I made that a ground for my break up. Most of me wanted to change her. Guess, I couldn't accept her as she was. So that's my story."

"Hmmm… You sound like a guy who is a gentleman secretly behind all your cool self. Why do you try so hard to be someone else?"

"I guess we all want to fit in and not be an outcast. I know I am one already but I am scared to let them know."

"Let me let you in on another secret. A girl might like any guy but she will only fall for the gentleman in that guy. Be yourself and I am sure you will have a beautiful love story in the days to come," said Miss.8

"Thank you, Miss. 8. So tell me more about your story. We have another five minutes with us."

"Nothing much to say. I hope to find a guy just like him," she answered.

The bell rang and 15 min had lapsed, but some tables were still going on with just one side of the tale yet to finish. But the next event was started. It dealt with knowing each other and their preferences.

Friction wagon it was titled. The pairs had to discuss about their preferences as a continuation of the previous story about exes.

Janaki and Raghav, on the other hand, were on war path. Raghav was not in a very good mood. Instead of salvaging the situation, he went full on, trying to put down Janaki's demands, labelling them as irrational and completely egoistic. The differences that never seemed to crop up all this while had suddenly surfaced from nowhere, and their relationship was ambushed. What had changed they knew not. Was it the impulsive trigger of maintaining supremacy or was it the fear of an unsatisfactory future? Things weren't well.

"So you cannot put up with me is what you mean?" blurted Janaki.

"I can't put up with your unrealistic demands in our relationship. You are very bossy. I have never seen you like this. This is clearly the worst day of my life. Only yesterday we met and had such a good time. I am what I am and you knew it all along," he yelled.

Janaki started crying and choking ultimately terminating the call. Raghav was equally worried that he had said many things he never meant to. But both their egos wouldn't let them call each other. They relived the entire conversation and did so in a loop completely losing their night to moments of inextricable sadness.

Raghav was in deep contemplation.

"Facebook had really brought my life and Krishna's life into tremendous scrutiny. We really need to mind what we put there. Everything put there is construed to be a reflection of us and to judge a person solely based on that seems completely unfair and foolish. How sure are you that people are what they claim to be? I may not put up what a good hearted guy I am for the fear of being called narcissist or a show off or just because I don't want to. But it's the most appropriate time for those people with their selfies and constant updates about their lives. No one likes to have things private anymore.

People check in if they went for a movie and also check in if they went for a mourning. Posting a picture to me of your empty breakfast plate and your early morning face with your unbrushed teeth wide open. I have to like it and comment like I have seen the Holy Grail. The ratio of the useful or friendly updates that go on FB or any social networking site for that matter versus the mundane, untrue, defamatory and exaggerated things that feature there should be made a point for moot. Might be FB should consider some option and change our hypocrisy. I bet we are not so good. Many wear masks and show themselves to be persons who they dream to be as opposed to whom they actually are and the opposite gender falls for it. I put out the truth and wearing my heart on my sleeves has got me into deep trouble. I better clear out all those things on FB and set my account straight to only the things which purely reflects me. No fake smiles or kind words. To say what I truly feel and to express myself genuinely has become oblivious to my manners and it's time I play myself. I like this drama and I am at best an actor who fits all characters except my own," he ended a little note that he wrote. Raghav worked as a magazine editor and the editor in him was happy about the next week hot story that had just dawned. He made a few calls and hoped to hear opinions and experiences of others. His mailbox was flooded with stories of the like.

Back at the blind date, the favourites had been written, and Krishna was surprised that most of their choices matched. Miss. 8 was an ardent lover of melodious music and violin instrumentals. Krishna himself preferred the jazz and was all for melodious music. Miss. 8 was an ardent devotee of Lord Shiva, and our man was not so serious about religion now but during his early days he marvelled at the stories and folklore that sung praises of

Lord Shiva. The lord of destruction was also the most charismatic and mystical to him.

His favourite place in the whole world he confessed was his home. So did Miss. 8. They even giggled frequently at each other becoming more aware of the commonalities between them. A little chemistry had magically found its way to their conversations.

"Hey, are you saying such things because you want to please me or are they true?" asked Miss. 8.

"Well, I have no clue who you are or how you look but I am already liking you a little," he confessed. "If I was the guy 2 years ago might be I would have said things to please you. But thanks to Kavya I have learnt never to introduce myself to anyone as someone who I am not to start with. I wish you have sparkling eyes Miss. 8. Just a testimony to my level of honesty at present," he informed.

Janaki was devastated in her own way unable to come to terms at the rude behaviour of Raghav. She was almost in sync with the study of personality traits that Radha had mooted.

She texted Radha "Had a fight with Raghav. I think it's beyond reconciliation. Where are you?"

Radha texted back "Please keep calm. Don't do anything stupid. Avoid any conversation until tomorrow. I will be back in a while and we shall discuss."

Janaki was browsing through the pictures taken with Raghav. They seemed a happy couple, and she was reminded of their time together which only deepened the pain of her helpless situation. She stuffed her wet eyes into a pillow unable to understand why Raghav had been so rude to her. They have had fights before but today was different. It was like he couldn't bear her question his character despite her knowing him so well. What had changed? Was she asking for more? or was his reaction to her questioning his integrity overdone?

The bell had rung for the second time. The story they began to narrate was half way through. They had known about what they liked in a person and what they disliked and ultimately whether they had similarity of tastes and if not whether they could reconcile their differences over tastes. There were discussions all through the hall. Some pairs had learnt that they were not meant for each other while in some pairs one of them was optimistic that they could make things work while the other wasn't. The learning of differences and being accommodative to partner's habits was a stumbling block in many of the already ended dates. The resilience to accept the differences of the partners has clearly diminished in the society one could think. Tailor making partners to each other's preference was kind of the in thing. The last round saw just three pairs actively participating. Numbers 13, 1 and 8. The others just sat around not to look rude. The last round was about where the story would go. The past and the present were examined in the previous rounds, and the last event just was left open to the pairs.

The finest hour came at table no. 8, when Miss. 8 excused herself to go and help her friend who was having a tough time in her relationship.

"So you are going to leave me alone here all by myself?"

"Yes, I have to. She needs me. I am really sorry. You seem like a really nice person. I wish I could have stayed for longer."

"Well, I don't know about you but I would love a great ending to this story in fact a fairy tale one."

Miss. 8 prompted "I am blushing yet again. You really talk sweet and I can say with certainty that you watch a lot of romcom movies. Are you a writer or something?

"Miss. 8 spot on. How did you know? Are you telepathic or something?"

"No, I found you use much similes and conjunctions in whatever you spoke. Also you sounded poetic now and then. There are only two people with such traits. One is the romantic and the other is a writer."

"So you are saying I don't sound like a romantic?"

"I am yet to see it. That's all. You also used certain words one could find only in a thesaurus."

"I believe some stories need to be continued. I hope this is such. Will I meet you again? Just to be clear I am being honest now," said Krishna.

"I guess you will know about it in a week if you get my call."

The arrangement was that the male partners would be given the contact number of the other if their partners decided to go on a second date.

"I really have to go now. I am really sorry, Mr. 8. Have a good eve," she greeted and swiftly rushed past Krishna.

Krishna rose half way up to send her off when he felt her saree brush past his face like the sweetest kiss. He could still feel and smell the sweet fragrance of her saree long after she was gone.

Radha reached her friend and enquired what had happened.

"I told you that this would happen Janaki. You said you felt connected. Such impulsive relationships mostly end with a bitter break up. Why don't you call and sort things out?" advised Radha.

"No, let him sort it out. It was he who was rude to me," replied a teary eyed Janaki.

"What? How could she say such things? Doesn't she know how much you love her? And why the hell did you have to blurt such things at her?" asked Krishna.

"If she had asked about me, I would have answered patiently. She spoke about her friend Radha not liking you based on your FB account and ultimately considering you a 'cynical hypocrite' and then she went on to question me. I felt a little taken aback when I understood she wasn't kidding with me and that she was serious about getting a reply. One thing led to another and I said things I shouldn't have."

"Why don't you call her and sort things out?"

"I have been most accommodative in our relationship. It's time she learns to be likewise. Let her call or let's just get done with it."

A week had passed and the wait was killing Krishna but he was equally worried that his friend was going to miss a really sweet girl over a petty quarrel. In the midst of all this, he was reading the newspaper sipping a cup of coffee when he received a text that revealed the contact information of Miss. 8. He jumped in joy screaming loud enough to wake Raghav. Raghav was elated to hear the news and wished him all luck.

The meeting was fixed in the Moonstar Café the same evening at 8 p.m.

Krishna had reached by 7:30 and waited to welcome Miss. 8. He had wild imaginations about how she would be. The dress was cream coloured saree, she had informed. He was gazing at the entrance for too long and had taken two loo breaks in a short expanse of time. His anxiety was very evident that the waiter asked him if he needed him to call the medic.

Radha walked in wearing a smashing cream-coloured saree, her dark skin still giving a mesmerizing shine and Krishna looked in complete disbelief at her. The reaction was similar at her end. Radha wondered whether to run away or to stay and excuse herself later. Krishna received a text right at that moment from Raghav.

"Janaki and I have broken up. I think I should have made that call you asked me to."

Radha received a text from Janaki revealing the break up. Radha walked in and greeted Krishna. Krishna started to speak slowly and clearly "Our friends need us now. What do you say about rekindling a little love and playing cupid for our friends?"

"No wonder I liked you. You are not so bad after all. I guess I was misdirected by the things I saw on your account in FB," said Radha her saree still sitting crisp on her resolute shoulders, her glasses given a miss and her eyes sparkling.

"I guess the story is going to get interesting then. What do you suggest we do to get the love birds back together?"

Janaki was asked to meet Radha at the café and similarly Raghav was asked to meet Krishna at the café. They had both feigned that they had a terrible fight with each other and that the other had stormed out of their meet. The café owner consented to a small drama of sorts which he informed will be filmed and marketed to advertise his café if there was a happy ending. The lights were made dim. Janaki had made a small video of them for Raghav's birthday earlier, and Radha had helped her and she had a copy of the same. They both entered the dim lit café and they met at the entrance. Janaki swiftly walked in unable to control her tears. Raghav followed with a dejected mood himself at the sight of Janaki. They both were surprised to see the video being played and when it ended their favourite song came up. All those moments of unadulterated love was relived.

The lights got brighter and they stood alone looking at each other, Janaki's tears melting Raghav. "I am sorry" placards were stuck all around the café. Raghav walked across to Janaki and apologized. Janaki had nothing to say for she was overwhelmed with feelings and fell into his arms as their differences were crushed by wonderful memories of their true inner feelings for each other. There were claps erupting from all ends of the café.

Two friends approached them from the darkest end of the café. They both thanked Krishna and Radha and wished them a joyful union if all goes well. Janaki was holding the hands of Raghav without letting go as if a long lost thing had just been found. Radha and Krishna bid goodbye to the lovebirds and left the café.

Krishna's mobile beeped "Janu's aunt hates roses." Radha's mobile beeped a little while later "Raghav's uncle likes you so much but he wouldn't confess it seems."

Krishna ditched the rose in his pocket.

"So I guess the night is still young, and the cupids have been really impressive. What do you think?" asked

Krishna removing his coat and placing it on Radha like a gentleman would.

"I think this story is going to have a great ending," she spoke and held the hand of Krishna.

"I think some stories preferably should never end," replied Krishna setting his first kiss on her dusky cheek.